MOTHER OF GOD

ALSO BY CAITLIN ELIZABETH

Everything in Between

PRAISE FOR CAITLIN ELIZABETH

Praise for *Everything in Between*

"What I thought was going to be a delightful romp through someone's personal travels, turned into a delightful romp through someone's personal trauma, travels, and revelations...and that's just what this book is... a revelation. I was completely entranced with the author's style and moments of enlightenment, all of which will live with the reader, examining their own journey through this thing we call life. A fantastic read!"

—Goodreads

"If I can be totally honest with you, I worry that you're going to get pushback for being a stereotypical, self-involved millennial."

—Literary agent

"I wish I could give this book more than five stars because it deserves it! This book is an excellent collection of essays about loving yourself, finding happiness, life lessons and traveling the world. It has wit, emotion and will make you feel all the feels! Highly recommend!!"

—My sister

"My biggest concern is you've never written a book before."

—Life coach

Praise for *Mother of God*

"I really loved this book. The characters have such vibrant personalities. I could totally hear their voices in my head! Can't wait to see it on the shelves."

—Early reader

"I love the voice of this book! I found myself drawn in by the premise, and your cute LGBTQIA story lured me right in."

—Literary agent

MOTHER OF GOD

a novel

caitlin elizabeth

ROSE WAY BOOKS

California

For my sister;
there are many sisters in this world,
but I'm so glad to be yours.

God is the love that moves the sun and the stars.

-Dante, The Divine Comedy

author's note

Growing up as a Catholic school girl, I learned how the *original* Christmas story was about a mother giving birth in a divisive political climate. She gave birth to a child who the government wanted to kill. The moral always stuck with me: On the darkest day with the least hope, love finds a way.

This book is a remembrance of that core message as well as a response to the general fuckery that's been happening in the world at large since then, especially in the recent years.

Ellie and Austin are a melting pot of all the things I—and so many of us—have been shamed for: our mental health, sexuality, gender expression, marital status, job title, or position within the nuclear family.

This book is for you, me, and anyone who has had to sit at a table, in a classroom, or in a relationship where love isn't being served. It's a reminder of the *true* meaning of the First Coming:

That the light always returns.
And love always wins.

part one:
the visitation

1

'I don't know if I'd ever be content getting married.'

Ellie (she/her) couldn't stop the words from spilling out. She swore she wouldn't spend the night, but here she is. *Again.* The thing is she just sleeps so well when she's in Pete's energy field. Like the part of her that's never gotten any rest can finally let go. But on this particular morning, she is naked, vulnerable, and feeling things—all dynamite for her self-sabotage instincts, which are clearly kicking in.

Pete (he/him, respectfully open) closes his eyes, knowing exactly what she's doing. 'Oh yeah, why's that?'

'Like Gloria said, *the surest way to be alone is to get married.*'

'I actually did a little research myself. She's since updated that theory. Here, let me find it.'

Reaching for his phone, Pete sweetly scrolls, looking for the words he *knows* will impress Ellie. However, his already-spoken words have set off alarm bells inside her body. The anxiety rushes from her ponytail to her toes as her internal panic alarm blares. *May Day. S.O.S. Emergency. Red alert. 911!!!! All hands on deck!*

Ellie met Pete at an underground rave in Oakland, except he was not the usual Bay Area guy (no padded vest, no fancy tech title). He had nothing to prove and no venture capital to be won. Of course, she was immediately intrigued (and insanely attracted). Over the years, they've been on and off, mostly thanks to her. She runs away, terrified of the connection, trying to force the switch to "off," for both of them. The problem is: Love doesn't work like that. Nothing about it can be forced.

Pete cutely smiles. 'Ah, here it is. And I quote: *Being married is like having somebody permanently in your corner. It feels limitless, not limited.* Gloria Steinem.'

Casually, Ellie attempts to brush this kind gesture right off, literally combing her hair to the side. 'I actually prefer her earlier writing.'

'I'm sure you do.' Slightly amused, Pete tries to embrace her, hoping some physical touch will clear the air.

But his hands only make Ellie more anxious, mostly because she knows he can read her like a book—and she's not in the mood to be read, right now.

Sensing her energy shift, Pete tries to de-escalate her insecurities. 'Look, it's not like I'm going to propose anytime soon, you can relax.'

Here we go. Ellie throws the covers off and hastily jumps to her feet. 'Oh, so what does that mean? You don't think I'm marriage material? Is it my profession? Or just because I'm an inferior WOMAN?' She briskly pulls her clothes on, determined to escape as quickly as possible. *Intimacy is a disaster and it always will be.*

'Whoa, whoa, whoa, whoa, okay, so you're *not* kidding. Hey, slow down please. For the record, I *was* just kidding, I could tell you were uncomfortable and-'

'No, no, it's fine, I get it. I know how you really feel, you don't need to MANSPLAIN it.'

'Ellie, come on, don't do this. Can we just put this to bed? Actually, come back to bed, I'll make it up to you.'

For a moment, she's tempted. But her worst instincts take over as she continues to scramble for her stuff, scattered across Pete's room.

'Who knew you were such an ADVOCATE for the patriarchy? Certainly not me!'

Pete can't help but laugh, even though he knows it's only adding gasoline to her fire. 'Hey, you know I've worked through my toxic masculinity stuff—you've helped me with that.'

She pauses for a moment, grateful for his humble admission. But her attachment style won't let her rethink this.

'*Please* come back to bed, Ellie, c'mon, this is crazy.'

That's it. She stops, slowly turning towards him. 'What did you just say?'

'Babe, okay, you know I didn't mean it like that.'

'What *did* you mean it like, then?'

'I just meant it, like, ugh shit, why are you doing this?'

'You know what, I'm glad this happened. I'm glad I got to hear how you really feel.'

'Ellie Jones, this is so unfair. You're not even listening to me.'

'Oh, does it anger you when someone won't listen to you, the person with a penis?!' Ellie storms towards the door, thinking twice before walking through it, only to scream, 'Well, guess what? We're done.' With that, she slams it shut, turns on her heels, and shouts behind her, 'For good this time.'

Pete sticks his face in his pillows. *Faccccccck. She's doing it. Again. She will be the death of him. Or at least his ego.*

As Ellie huffs down the stairs to the outside world, she thinks the same thing. So many parts of her want to turn around and apologize, but instead, she lets her lowest part lead the way, away from love. *Fuck. Maybe she will check out her mom's YouTube channel, after all.*

2

Getting down the Embarcadero is hell on a Saturday night. The whole road gets clogged up with Teslas, all driving themselves as their owners pound away on their laptops, even on the weekend.

Sometimes it feels like Ellie is in *The Jetsons* as she sits on MUNI, watching the tech bros breeze by, with their hands on tablets, instead of the wheel. She's probably crossed paths with (at least) one of them this fiscal year, statistically speaking, at *her* place of work.

So many people judge her because she doesn't have a "respectable, society-approved" job. But honestly, her body has been judged, watched, lusted after, and groped ever since her chest first popped. *She might as well cash in on it, for fuck's sake.*

Ironically, when she arrives in the Financial District, the streets are eerily quiet. *Probably because everyone is working from their cars?* She heads straight to the back alley and lights up. The back door to her place of work swings open with a loud thud, causing Ellie to jump. *Will capitalism ever give her a moment of peace?*

Luckily, it's not her boss. Just her fellow comrade, Rosa (she/her, for now). She makes more than anyone else in the club by taking pictures of her toes, along with catering to a revolving door of daddies, most of whom request to be humiliated by her, in a shocking mutation of their male-dominated culture.

Nudging Ellie, Rosa lights a joint. 'I think Grandma is calling tonight.'

Confused, Ellie takes a drag. 'What? Gigi calls me ten times a day, you know that.'

'Not *her*. THE Grandmother.'

'Like from *Moana*? I'm lost.'

'I *mean*, it's time to try the *Vine of the Dead*. Do I have to spell it out for you?'

Finally, it hits Ellie. 'Ohhhh, yeah. Duh!'

Rosa looks at her, deadpanned. 'Did you cleanse?'

'Yes, of course.'

In reality, Ellie did not do one second of cleansing. If anything, her intake of off-limit substances increased *exponentially* over the past week. *Whatever, it'll be fine.*

Tap. Tap. Tap. The window above them opens.

'What are you doing, losers?'

There's nothing that irritates Ellie more than being interrupted. Especially by someone like Jake (he/him), their manager. A *where's my hug?* kinda guy. He caddies at a golf course in Lake Merced by day, and then shows up here, horny and covered in grass stains, ready to manage "his girls." He's had a crush on Ellie since she first started and has been sure to let her know. *Ick.*

From the window above, he smiles like a cat who spotted a bunch of unprotected mice. 'Welcome back, ladies. Get inside, it's freezing out there. Love that hair Ellie - hah!'

* * *

In the locker room, Ellie rushes through her routine. Pasties on, lacy crop top over the head, liquid eyeliner on her lids, a quick scan of the motivational post-its on her locker door, fishnet tights around her ankles as she takes the (mandatory) pregnancy test in a stall, styling her newly dyed mane of pink into pigtails, adding glitter to her cheeks and just everywhere, pulling her favorite silver stilettos on her feet, pounding two glasses of water, and done.

As expected, the test is negative. *Would have to be a true Immaculate Conception.* Pete is always safe, about everything. *Especially, insemination.*

She needs her security blanket, so she starts hastily typing:

I need to get out of here.

AUSTIN: Where are you? Are you ok?!

Ellie and Austin (he/him publicly, she/they privately) grew up next door to each other across the Bay in Belvedere. A town that is exactly one square mile, surrounded on three sides by water, and has the most wealth per square inch in northern California. A level of privilege most people will never experience. But for Ellie and Austin, they might as well have grown up on Alcatraz. They both spent their childhoods dreaming about moving into the city, fantasizing of diving into the urban landscape together, with broken things and horny people and dumpsters. And they did just that. The moment they turned eighteen, the duo practically swam across the Bay, making a break for it like two prisoners who had been planning their escape route for decades.

Quickly, Ellie rethinks her approach. The last time she expressed a hint of distress, Austin sprinted from the Castro through the Tenderloin in the middle of the night, risking their life and their Prada purse. She doesn't want to endanger them like that again.

Yes, sorry. You still okay with picking me up later?

AUSTIN: Of course, Miss Daisy. Can't wait to chauffeur you home from the astral plane.

'LADY!!! CALL OUT!!!' Jake pokes his head through the locker room door, even though he's not supposed to, clearly trying to get a peek.

Ellie screams back, 'Coming!'

She does a triple-check of her body. Pasties, lacy crop top, eyeliner, pigtails, glitter, stilettos. She tops it all off with her embroidered jacket, featuring her dancer name on the back. *Lady Jane.* She always wanted one of these letter jackets in her teen years, but she wasn't "popular" or "good at sports" or a "team player." *Suck on this, high school.*

'LADY!! NOW! YOU'VE GOT TEN SECONDS!! ONE-TWO-TEN!'

Approaching the door, she pulls her jacket around her a little tighter, shielding her body from her boss's gaze. 'Jesus, I'm right here.'

'It's with your favorite.'

Jake gestures over his shoulder to the elderly man standing a few feet behind him, eagerly awaiting Ellie's arrival. Sometimes old men don't just want a dance, they want the "girlfriend experience."

Ellie's heart sinks. 'Can't Rosa go this time?' She gestures over her shoulder to Rosa, who is filming another lucrative foot video for her "fans."

Jake shakes his head, leaning in for (another) hug attempt. 'We both know you're more Dick's type.'

Ellie brushes past him. 'That's what he said.'

At least this much older gentleman caller, aptly named Dick (not her grandpa - he/him), is (mostly) respectful. He worked in insurance for decades, until an unfortunate accident with a fax machine lost him a finger but gained him a fortune. He's since developed an unhealthy obsession with spending his money at the club, particularly on Ellie. He truly loves taking her on dates, and she's starting to think he believes they are *actually* dating. *At least he tips well.*

Dick always insists on taking her to The Stinking Rose, an old school Italian restaurant up the street. She usually resists because she hates reeking like garlic afterwards. But tonight, she's starving and can't wait to go to town on the most garlic-filled item on the menu.

Together, they share a table, decorated in a tacky, red-checkered tablecloth, in the back room for regulars, away from the tourists. It's weird how she'll go on dates with clients, but hates going anywhere with anyone she *actually* likes, who is not paying for her services. Like Pete. *Should she apologize? A topic to unpack with her therapist.*

The waiter approaches, with one of those big silly-looking garlic hats on his head, as Dick starts playing footsie with her under the table.

'And what will you two be having?'

Ellie deflects even being asked what she wants to eat. 'Oh, um, this is my grandpa.'

Dick smiles and reaches for her hand as the waiter tries to hide his skepticism.

'Sure. Alright then, for you, Sir?'

Always the gentleman, Dick responds. 'Ladies first.'

Ellie knows her idol would be pounding her fists on the table; the misogyny is stankier than the garlic in this place. 'So sweet. I'll have the chick, I mean the chicken.'

Dick can't keep his hands to himself, slapping the side of her ass. 'Good for you, Lady. Let's put some meat on those bones.'

Ignoring the glaring sexism but picking up on the vibe, the waiter continues. 'Let me guess, a hunk of meat for you, Sir?'

Bingo! Dick has a shit-eating grin on his face while he cuts into his T-bone as Ellie houses her entire entrée. She's antsy as she waits for him to make his way through the steak, knowing he has to take it slow, what with his dentures and all.

They've made it through most of the meal without any outbursts, and she's finally feeling herself relax a bit. Enough to start some conversation.

'How's your steak?'

'Juicy, like you.'

'That's...hot.'

Dick smiles, taking a few more bites before he slams his silverware down. 'I have a BONER!'

Fuck. Ellie should have known better. Why did she have to say 'that's hot'? She has to stop watching *The Simple Life* before bed.

'Okay, okay. Calm down.'

The waiter approaches slowly, sliding the check towards Dick, while

Ellie shoots him a look of gratitude. *Can work be over now, please?*

When they exit the restaurant, she gives Dick a peck on the cheek, and then feels the urge to puke as he walks away. She's not sure if it's from the garlic, the misogyny, or what. All she knows is something feels a little off, like inside her. She's just not quite sure what it is, yet.

3

The first thing she notices is the Amazon rainforest decor. *This has to be appropriation of some kind.* Apparently, this underground "jungle" experience was the brainchild of some tech geniuses, who knew the higher ups in the digital world wanted to go to South America, but were not allotted the time, so they simply brought Peru to the Bay. *As one does.*

Luckily, within three seconds, Ellie spots Rosa with their other fellow worker, Stacey (she/they), who decided to join in "the trip" last minute. *Either a wonderful decision or a horrible one…only time will tell!* Stacey is posh as hell but does not want to be. She ran away from her affluent East Coast family in a luxury SUV, driving it straight across the country and never looking back. She only works with Ellie and Rosa for fun, purely out of rebellion.

The colleagues sit on yoga mats before a shaman who claims to be Peruvian (but seems suspiciously North American), as he prepares the medicine in a cauldron. Ellie gets a sixth sense that something is "off" with this guy. First, he's wearing a fake wolf's head. Second, he keeps mumbling about high vibrations and dark energies. And third, she's pretty sure she's given him a private dance before.

Finally, the shaman speaks. 'How do you girls know each other?'

Stacey shoots back. 'We're in a church group together.'

Something in this exchange triggers him, probably because he knows they're not telling the truth. But (*surprise, surprise*) neither is he. He is *not* an actual shaman. He simply took one free webinar online and has never actually administered medicine to anyone, ever before. This will be a first for all of them.

'Wonderful. Please lay down on your backs and get comfortable.'

Ellie has the strong urge to mess with him, smelling his bullshit from a yoga mat away.

'We'll be drinking the…Miss Ellie, did you already drink yours?'

Showing no signs of remorse, Ellie swallows the last drop. 'Oh yeah. Sorry, I took down the whole thing.'

The shaman is pissed and his overpronouncing in a South American accent reaches new heights. 'Alright, that was for ALL THREE of you. I strongly recommend you purge your system.' He points to a bucket in the corner.

Ellie shrugs him off. 'No worries. I'll be fine. I'm excited to see what the buzz is about.'

Stacey interjects. 'You're going to LOVE it.' She's been dabbling in psychedelics since she was twelve, in various locations around the Upper East Side.

'You've done this before?'

'Of course, darling.'

* * *

Ten minutes later, Stacey is puking her brains out in the bucket as she urgently inquires, 'Was this organically curated? Are there any synthetics in this blend?'

Meanwhile, Rosa is in a deep state of meditation, almost as if she's sleeping. *Or heavily drugged.*

Over on the other yoga mat, Ellie is stiff as a board, not light as a feather. Her vision keeps going in and out of focus, and she's not sure whether to ride this wave, or freak the fuck out.

Music will help. She pulls out her phone, mostly to drown out the humming this "shaman" won't stop doing. The first thing she sees is an email from her mom.

Subject: You're Invited to a Coming Out Party!

Dear Faithful Friends and Family,

I'm hosting a celebration next Sunday after mass. Father Tom will be giving a short presentation on the church's guidelines for LGBTQ+ issues.

Come one, come all! All races, sexes, and genders included - IN THIS HOUSE, WE DO NOT DISCRIMINATE!

Please wear something colorful (we're taking back the rainbow - it's for everyone!)

Reminder: As people of faith, we must tolerate all kinds.

Also, this event is BYOG – Bring Your Own Gay! :)

Oh, for the love of god. Of course, her mother has somehow commandeered her life, once again, throwing this party in yet another attempt to figure out who Ellie is sleeping with?! *How bizarre.*

Ellie compartmentalizes the invite, shoving the email into her mental file of "Things My Mother Does that I Must Repress in Order to Function" as she closes her eyes, plugs in her headphones, and puts her latest playlist on shuffle. She'll let the universe decide what song she needs to hear.

Pretty quickly, Ellie starts feeling better. Cheery. Happy-go-lucky. Delighted, even. One of her favorite songs comes on, full blast. It's actually quite meaningful to her and feels synchronistic. For once, it doesn't make her feel sorrowful, but…joyful? The music carries her away, to another world…

* * *

The vision is blurry at first, like she's walking through dense fog that suddenly clears, finding herself in a field of lavender. The sky is full of fluffy pink clouds, and she's wearing a beautiful free-flowing skirt (with pockets!), as if Mother Earth picked out her outfit of the day.

Feeling the grass beneath her feet, she reaches a clearing with a white cotton blanket spread across the ground and a chilled glass of lemonade, waiting just for her. Quickly chugging the whole glass, she notices a visitor.

'So good, right?'

Alarmed, Ellie scooches back on the blanket, weirded out by this ethereal stranger. Sure, it's one of the most beautiful people she's ever seen, a beauty that shines well beyond labels. And they're glowing, almost like…an angel. But still, she's uneasy.

'Are you…?'

'A hot, gorgeous angel starring in your ayahuasca vision? Yes, I am. And I'm here to see you today, girlfriend.'

Ellie starts to panic. 'No, no, no. I think you have the wrong person. Not me. Must be someone else.'

The angel plops down next to her, slightly annoyed. 'No reason to fear. It's definitely you I'm here for. Ellie Jones, virgin, 33 years old, pink hair, scheduled to be in a warehouse off the Embarcadero tonight with two friends and a quack shaman.'

'Okay, no, *none* of that describes me, you *definitely* have this all wrong! I'm *not* a virgin, in any sense.'

'I meant the *real* definition of virgin, not how you Earthlings use it. Like as in pure of heart, a free person, independent, sexually and otherwise. That is you, no?'

'Okay, I'm not interested in whatever it is you're selling, so, no thank you! This is really creepy.'

The angel meets her at eye level, taking her hands in theirs. 'Honey, there's no reason to fear, I'm simply here to remind you of what you've forgotten.'

'I have no idea what you're talking about.'

'I'm afraid you do, though.'

With that, the vision shape shifts and now, she's in Golden Gate Park, lying on the grass, holding…a baby? As she stares into the baby's eyes, she wants to squeeze them close and hold them forever. The chubby cheeks, the rolls on the legs, the little feet. And the baby smell. She has never, ever, in her life, loved anyone, anything, any moment, as much as this one. The love pours over her, washing through her soul, like nothing she's ever felt before. And then, she hears the angel's voice.

'You must agree to love this child with all your heart, no matter what happens.'

Screaming with all her might, Ellie relents. 'Yes, okay, yes, yes, yes! YES!!!!!'

Back in the warehouse, the shaman and Stacey exchange a glance, not sure what kind of vision Ellie is having, but it appears to be a pleasant one.

The angel now looks at her with seriousness. 'Love is not always easy. But you were chosen for this.'

As Ellie ponders something, she finally asks. 'Okay wait, can I ask a logistical question? What do I do when the baby is born though? About the private parts?'

'Ew, okay. The obsession you all have with the genitalia of babies is really, really weird. Not you honey, just the world in general. It's nobody's business what is in your child's diaper.' The angel pauses, thinking for a little. 'Just follow the signs and everything will be okay.'

Skeptically, Ellie looks at the angel, but she still nods. If there's anything she believes in, it's signs from the universe.

The angel gives her a big hug, leaving her with one last piece of advice. 'Okay, I'm sorry to do this. This next part isn't going to tickle, but just remember, you're never alone. Good luck, goddess speed, and I'll be watching over you, we all will…'

With that, the vision swiftly changes. Back in the park, she's holding her baby, but now, a police officer has entered the picture, grabbing at her child, trying to take them away. And it's not just any cop. It's her uncle.

She starts screaming her head off, both in the vision (and in real life). 'No, no, Uncle Timothy, this baby is mine. I'm the mother, I told you that already. Bloody hell, you're acting like a real bellend! Just stand down…Wait, wait, WAIT!'

As her screams of pleasure transform into desperate cries for help, Stacey checks in with the shaman. He has become as useless as a deflated life raft, sitting back on his mat, filing his nails, vaguely motioning for everyone to stand back. Rosa couldn't be less bothered too, mostly because she seems to be comatose, a whole other issue in itself.

After a few more seconds of Ellie writhing on the floor in agony, the shaman ceremoniously gets up, swiftly removing her headphones. *Not the right move.* She freaks out, even more, screaming profanities at her uncle.

'Fuckshitballsackhomiehopperassholerepublicandamncrapbloodyhellhol ycowtwatdickhead. Nooooo!!!! NOOOOO!!!! I need my baby back, give me my baby back!! I told you, I'm the mother. Get Gigi, she'll tell you, she knows!'

The shaman tries to get Ellie to calm down. But she squirms, panicking with her eyes now wide open, screaming bloody murder. The halluci- nation is no longer separate from real life. It's all blurred together, in a swirl of blended realities. After some more moments of heaving and sobbing, Ellie gets a renewed sense of strength as she pops up from the floor, looks the shaman dead in the eye, throws her hands in the air, and releases a deeply visceral howl:

'GLORRRRRRRRIIIIIIAAAAAAAAAA!!!!!!!!'

4

A few tokens tell Ellie where she is, every day. Namely, the sign on the wall for "Behavioral Health Unit" spells it out loud and clear. But in case she forgets, the tray of food with baby utensils, nothing to hurt anyone, is a reminder. And the special toilet in the bathroom. And the bedroom with only a table and a bed. Plastic sheets, even.

Weirdly, she's found there are some things to like about this place. Art time is great, she likes painting. Especially finger painting. High-fiving other patients under the *No Touching* sign has been a bit of a rush too, especially if her favorite nurse is around.

Maisie (she/her) has worked in the psych ward for most of her adult life, underappreciated and underpaid the whole time. All she wants is enough money to buy a house with a garden in Guerneville for her girlfriend. And she is *more* than fed up with people like Ellie and their entitled shit. When she caught Ellie trying on a straitjacket in the storage closet one afternoon, she'd had enough. So, she packed her schedule to the brim, mostly with the activity she hates the most. The absolute worst part of living in the ward, for Ellie, is group therapy. *Barf.*

* * *

Sitting in a circle with the other residents, Ellie bounces her baby doll (aptly named Gloria) on her lap. She sits across from Moseby (they/them), the therapist who would best be described as very dry and really cool. In truth, Moseby is sick, weary even, of being the only person in the room who has evolved beyond outdated gender norms. *It's exhausting.* Of course, Ellie instantly felt an affinity towards them. When Moseby told her how their own family tried to send them to a conversion camp to "get the gay out," it was at *that* moment that she decided that she must defy the rules and make Moseby her friend.

There's a new person in today's circle, a punk femme with purple and black hair—and Ellie wants to make her like her too. Like, *like* her like her. They keep eyeing each other so the feeling *might* be mutual. *Maybe she will find love here...*

Moseby gestures towards the purple-haired beauty. 'Why don't you go first?'

Miserae (she/her) looks away, pretending not to notice she's being addressed. Eventually, she realizes she can't ignore it. 'What do you want to know?'

Moseby clears their throat, trying to command control. 'Let's start with your first name?'

'Pass.'

'Okay, it says here that your name is… Misa…Misery?'

Miserae is not amused. 'It's pronounced MISAH-RAY.'

Ellie (softly) chimes in. 'Loves it.'

Taking a deep breath, Moseby carries on. 'Okay, we'll come back to you, Miserae. Who would like to go next?'

Like a lightning bolt, Ellie shoots her hand up in the air.

'Anyone?' Moseby desperately scans the circle.

Defeated, they turn to Ellie and nod.

'Hi, I'm Ellie, she slash her. I really like pink. Like I'm obsessed with it. Hence, today's look.' She is dressed from head-to-toe, from her gown to her grippy socks, in pink, all of which she dyed in the sink, much to Maisie's horror.

'Great. When was the first time you felt shame?'

'Well, recently, actually. Before last week, I've been mostly pretty shame*less*, to be honest. You see, I have a full-time job...as an accountant.'

Ellie takes quick stock of the room. The judgment passes through the group like a wave. There's only one older gentleman who doesn't participate in the exchanged glances. Instead, he (Ellie thinks?) looks more like a protective masculine figure. *Now that's hot…*

She goes on. 'I took a little extra tip money to go on a trip, like a drug one, not a vacation.'

This declaration has greatly triggered Daniel (he/him) who has been holding in his frustration, until this moment when he finally combusts.

'Accountants do NOT get tips!!!'

Daniel is never not wearing a trench coat. His teachers and peers assumed he was heading down the path of a serial killer. Really, he's just a little undiagnosed and impulsive, but with a great heart. His parents both work full-time in tech and he was raised by hired help, only waving hello and sometimes goodbye to his mom and dad, every day for most of his life. All he wants is to be seen. And heard. *Definitely heard.*

But Ellie doesn't appreciate being talked over, especially by someone who identifies as a cisgender male. Or a cissy, as she calls them.

'Sir, I *am* an accountant.'

Moseby is annoyed with both of them. 'Please let's refrain from *only* using gender to identify ourselves and each other. Ellie, it's your turn to share.'

'As I was saying before I was *so rudely* interrupted…I took my profession-ally earned money from my abundant accounting business and I went to this healing center, which was really just an abandoned warehouse, like the ones you always wonder about along the Embarcadero. Well, wonder no more, people are definitely doing drugs in them. Anyway, I was with my girlfriends. Like my friends, I'm not dating them but I'm also not against dating a girl, I mean a woman, I mean a female. If you haven't guessed, I'm bi or maybe pan, if I had to put a label on it.'

No one is paying any attention. Ellie notices.

'Right. So, I'm proud to say, I took the ayahuasca down like a champ, but it didn't exactly sit well with me. So, here is the weird part. I had this, what I *now* know was a "fantasy"…but actually, this very *real* experience, for me, of being a MOTHER. It's quite ironic, really, given all my mommy issues. And daddy issues.'

'You can just say parent.'

'Right, my parental issues. But yeah, I genuinely thought someone had stolen my baby. And I did not take that...well.'

The other patients are either spacing out or giving Ellie a death glare in return. Or both. A slow, painfully awkward silence follows. *For one-Harry Styles, two-Harry Styles, three-Harry Styles, four-*

Until Ellie blurts out, 'It's all a big misunderstanding, on my end, really. And obviously, I know Timothée Chalamet is *not* the father, but goddess willing, maybe one day he will be.' Ellie crosses her fingers, shaking them to the gods and goddesses. During intake, she had begged the check-in desk to call her crush, the actor Timothée Chalamet, to straighten this whole mess out, claiming he had paternal rights to the baby she *didn't* have. Obviously, mentioning his name only solidified her stay in the mental ward.

Moseby continues their line of questioning, the only person other than Daniel, Miserae, and the older gentleman paying attention. 'How do you feel right now? Sharing this?'

Miserae unexpectedly chimes in. 'I feel nauseous.'

Finally, the man who's been observing Ellie inserts himself. 'I think it's very brave of Ellie to be so honest. It sounds like she will be a great mother one day.'

Ellie is taken aback, making a mental note to meet this mystery supporter later.

Moseby puts their hand over their heart. 'Have you thought about if you want to have children one day?'

Ellie tosses the question back, smacking it like a tennis ball right over the net. 'I am a child.'

Daniel can't help himself. 'That is not a lie.'

Moseby finally shows a bit of frustration. 'Please hold the commentary. Remember, your gender doesn't give you a free pass to comment whenever you please.' Turning their attention back to Ellie, Moseby continues. 'No, actually, you're an adult. Do you want to be a parent?'

'Ummmm I've never really thought about it? You know, lord knows I'd probably mess it up as bad as my parents did, and I'm just not sure that's worth the risk.'

'Go on.'

'Like, in front of...everyone?'

'Yes.'

'I mean, I gotta sort *this* out first. Love you all, but this isn't exactly where I pictured myself when I made my vision board, you know what I mean?'

Miserae finally agrees, for once. 'Amen to that.'

'I need to get my finances sorted and...'

Uh oh. Daniel perks up. 'I thought you were an accountant, though?'

'Um, yes, but I'm so busy helping everyone *else* with their money, that...'

'Ughhhhh, she's lying!! I knew she was LYING! She is NOT an accountant!!'

'How dare you doubt me, Sir!'

Exasperated, Daniel runs full speed out the door, while everyone else suddenly comes to life, like mummies rising from the dead, turning to stare at the exit, longingly, wishing they could make a run for it too.

5

By dawn, Ellie was out the door too. Most people would never have the uterus to break out, but finding a way out has always come naturally to her, like a sixth sense. She can escape any situation, no matter where she is, and she's never afraid to do it. *San Quentin is right down the creek, maybe she'll give that a go. Something to add to her bucket list.*

Upstream outside *the other* Bay Area prison, as she finally reaches the water, she lets out a little sigh and peels off her grippy socks. Sitting on her favorite fallen tree branch, she dips her feet in the water, which glimmers in the rising sun. Nature is healing, and there's nothing worse than being locked away from it. Although, losing access to her oracle cards has been rough. But sitting here, as the morning sunlight mixes with the fog, has become her new favorite ritual. *Who knew?*

Except she's not alone. Across the water, a mama deer and her two little ones each take a drink, gulping the water down. Instantly, she remembers the story her grandmother used to tell her before bed:

During the winter, when the days were getting shorter and darker, the animals felt cold, hungry, and hopeless. They knew something had to change, but no one wanted to travel to the Sun and ask it to come back. Until, a mother deer volunteered and was like, I'll go! She flew across the dark night sky, grabbing the Sun in her antlers, leaving a trail of sparkles as she brought light back to the land.

Of course, this ancient tale was co-opted by a man named Santa who became the star of the show. *Surprise, surprise!* But seeing this real life mother deer makes Ellie wonder if *all* mothers would go to the sun and back for their kids. Would she, if she ever *really* were a mom? *Probably.*

As if to confirm her answer, the mama deer looks up, making direct eye contact. Something about this moment feels both tender and intrusive. Like this mother is saying: *Of course you would. Now, you can watch us, but mess with my little ones and you're f'ing dead.*

A rustling in the bushes startles Ellie. Until she turns to see Austin approaching, wearing the same outfit Ace Ventura wore during his classic visit to the psych ward, tutu and all. A bold choice, but they are determined to lighten Ellie's spirits, no matter the cost. The besties have always supported each other in their lowest moments. And ironically, they've been coming to this spot down by the creek since high school, to get stoned. Back then, sometimes they'd even swim, even though their parents warned them they'd die of poisoning from the bay water. But they didn't. They both survived, only to end up back here, years later, like this—one in the psych ward and the other dressed like it.

Within two minutes, Austin sparks up a joint, just like the good old days, and asks the million-dollar question. 'Timothée Chalamet, huh?'

'I knew you'd like that.'

'Honey, he is prime baby daddy material. The moment I heard that, I knew you were going to be just fine. Any sane person would pick him.'

'At least I still have good taste, even when I'm breaking from reality.'

Smiling, they both let the silence fill the air, like a blanket of comfort.

Ellie finally asks the billion-dollar question. 'How's the family taking all this? Is everyone excited like: *I told you so! We've always known she was nuts!!*'

'Um, we both know that most of them belong here more than you do.'

'True.'

'How are you *really* doing, though?'

'Honestly, I'm hornier than I've ever been in my life.'

'Hah. Of course you are. You're the only person I know who would get turned on here.'

Austin sincerely points to their own chest, holding their heart. 'I meant, what's going on in here?'

Ellie doubles down. 'I *knew* you would notice! Yes, they *have* gotten bigger, thank you!'

'Okay, your tits do look great, even under that smock you're wearing, but we both know I want those for myself, so humble yourself.'

Austin knows Ellie is not ready to go deep, so they let her be. For now.

'ELLIE!!! I KNOW YOU'RE OUT HERE! You have ten seconds to get back here! ONE, TWO, TEN!'

Dammit. Maisie shows up to work thirty minutes early, every day. *Who comes to work early? It's not like they're paying her more!*

'Fuck, fuck, fuck. Go, go, go!'

Austin sprints their way down the creek path as Ellie takes one long, last rip, carefully putting the joint out and back in a plastic bag, tenderly tucking it under a log. As she slowly exhales, letting the cloud of smoke fill the air, Maisie pops up behind her.

'It's just fog, I swear!'

The mother deer leads her children away. *Humans are not a good example. No thanks.*

6

'I have a confession to make.'

Moseby gestures for Ellie to go ahead. 'Please.'

'I'm not an accountant.'

'I know.'

'I'm a dancer. I use my childhood nickname as my stage name. There, you know everything about me. Can I go now?'

'Thank you for being honest with me. Let's talk about why you're here.'

While leaning back on the couch in Moseby's office, Ellie appears un-phased as she creates new designs in the sand zen garden for fingers. Moseby remains professional but is clearly a little annoyed.

'Well, I didn't have much of a choice. My family wants me to stay. They've been telling me I need "help" for a while.'

'Why do they say that?'

'Because I'm different from them. I live a different lifestyle, I guess you could say.'

'How are you different?'

'I don't subscribe to the same value system they do. I don't go to church on Sundays, I've never been married, I'm not *totally* heterosexual, I don't have children…yet, I don't work a job they approve of, I'm stay-ing in San Francisco, instead of moving to southern California with them, what else…'

'I hear you. Let's switch gears. I'd like to talk about your notebook.'

'I don't know what you're talking about.'

'The one you keep in your room.'

Looking Moseby directly in the eye, Ellie challenges them. 'Don't know the one, does not ring a bell.'

Moseby gets up and walks to their desk, opening a drawer and pulling out the journal as Ellie's face freezes in horror.

'Where did you get that?! Is *nothing* in this world sacred anymore?'

Moseby had to crouch under Ellie's hospital bed this morning, sticking their arm under as far as they could, before pulling out the notepad. They open it to the first page and start scanning through.

'Did you write all this?'

'Fine, yes. That's my work.'

They keep thumbing through the pages, until finally closing it and handing it back to Ellie, who now sits with it carefully cradled in her lap, as she realizes she forgot her "baby" back in her room. *Hopefully they're doing okay...*

'Can you tell me what you're writing about?'

'No. Absolutely not. You are really crossing my boundaries.'

Moseby points to the journal. 'Did you buy that for yourself?'

'No, it was a gift. See, every year in December, people wrap up little boxes and give them to each other and you can tell how much a person loves you by how much money they spent on what's inside the box.'

Moseby simply looks at her. 'Let's switch gears. How is your relationship with your mother?'

'It's not great. Could be better.'

'What makes you think that?'

'It doesn't matter what I think. It's just the way it *is*.'

'And how *is* it? Between you and your mom?'

Ellie holds eye contact. 'Look, you don't have to convince me there's something wrong with me, my mother made sure I learned that. Early. Don't worry.'

'Can you give me an example?'

'Sure.' Ellie pauses for once, considering. 'In high school, there was this kid who lived on my street, Adam. Varsity soccer player, president of the student council, parents loved him. Anyway, my mom went on vacation, without me of course. She shipped me to my dad's and hired Adam to house-sit. He threw a three-day rager and the worst part? He didn't even invite me! When my mom got back, guess who she blamed? I was grounded for months, until Adam finally confessed. He later asked me to prom and called me a slut when I said no. And now he's the CEO of a tech startup, constantly being praised for being such a "good guy." My mom never apologized to me, and never has, for anything. So yeah, that's how she is. The first to crucify me, whether I'm innocent or guilty.'

Moseby holds a thoughtful pause. 'Love doesn't have to come from your birth parent. It can come from other people in your life.'

'Yeah, I mean, I have Gigi. I'm close with her.'

Moseby looks at her. They know Ellie will do anything to avoid talking about the things that hurt.

'Well, I know you'll be sad to hear this, but unfortunately, that's all the time we have for today.'

'No worries, and hey, if you ever need to reschedule, I'm okay with that. We can even just say I came and you can get paid and we can wrap all this up.'

'That will never happen.'

'It could.'

'It will not. See you next time, Ellie.'

7

Ellie feels ecstatic to find herself seated alone at a lunch table with Miserae, who feels the opposite. Of course, this only makes Ellie more determined to connect, on any level.

'So, what're you in here for?'

'Really?'

'Sorry, is that too personal?'

No response.

'Well, I like your hair!'

'Do you?'

'Yeah, I really do. No cap.'

'What the fuck does that mean?'

'You know, like, I'm not lying.'

'All you do is lie.'

Loving the snarky banter, Ellie tosses it right back. 'Aren't you a charmer?'

'Sorry.' Miserae runs her fork through the soupy peas, the cardboard mashed potatoes, and the turkey that looks plastic. 'I just really hate it here.'

Ellie nods. 'I get it. Things could be better.'

'You know, I thought you were a bitch when I first met you.'

'Please, tell me how you really feel!'

'You were just so...blonde. Even though your hair is pink, you still give off this Barbie vibe.'

'I get that a lot. But if it's any consolation, I was in the midst of a psychotic break.'

'You didn't look like it.'

'Most of us don't.'

At that moment, Daniel lets out a long grunt, as he frantically plays *Battleship* against himself, in total distress.

Ellie thinks for a moment. 'Okay, some of us do.'

* * *

On the way to group fitness hour, Daniel corners Ellie. 'Hey, I just want to let you know that there's this new girl coming today who is SUPER mean. I don't want her to hurt you.'

'Why would she do that?'

'Because I asked her to.' He pauses, staring at her, dead serious. 'Just kidding! C'mon, let's DANCE!'

Ellie conquered her phobia of group physical activity quite quickly. Usually, the patients are forced to do Tae Bo, like the videotape from the 90s, starring Billy Blanks. But she decided to teach the group her "famous" dance number. In middle school, she and Austin were suspended for performing a rousing, explicit number to *My Humps* at the annual talent show. Very *Little Miss Sunshine*, only their families did *not* join them on stage (although Gigi tried). Now, Ellie is convinced the dance has a (second) chance at going viral. Sponsorships from American Eagle and Dunkin' Donuts kinda viral.

'Okay, it's 5-6-7-8, whatcha gon' do with all that junk, twirl, step, all that junk inside that trunk? Daniel, from the top!'

Just as Daniel presses play, Ellie feels a familiar sensation, one she hasn't felt in a while. Her senses heighten and like a dog sniffing the air, she realizes danger is…near.

The music starts and within twenty seconds, her mom comes strutting down the hallway. Like a smoke alarm going off somewhere in her being, Ellie (immediately) drops to the ground.

Daniel does not like this. 'Get up, girl! We need you!'

'I'm taking a breather, don't mind me, I'm gonna just hang out here for a beat, it feels nice on my fists.'

Frustrated, Daniel pauses the music and nudges Ellie to get up. 'No one wants to see your W.A.P.!'

'Alright, alright, start the music again, I'm gonna do the rest on my knees…'

The moment Sue (refuses to claim pronouns) enters the doorway, she spots her daughter face down on the ground. She is the self-proclaimed "most successful life coach in California." Her self-help videos have inspired her to become more of a #BossMom. Who needs therapy when YouTube has so many experts and *YOU* are one of them?! (*Self-declared, of course*).

'Elizabeth Rosalind Jones, get on your feet right now!'

Ellie ignores her, so Sue comes over to the speaker, ripping the cord from the outlet just as Daniel presses play again.

Standing up, Ellie finally speaks. 'Everyone, the woman who groomed me for this place.'

8

Apparently, there was a family visit scheduled that no one told her about a.k.a. her karma for doing drugs in front of deer children.

Sitting atop her hospital bed, Ellie isn't sure who is the most uncomfortable. Her mom, Sue, sits on a chair in the corner, with her jacket on her lap, like a shield, looking as if she's trying to hold in a bowel movement while also wildly overdressed, per usual.

Her dad, Stan (he/him), is in a rolling chair by the door, on the opposite side of the room from his ex, head down, looking at his phone as if he's cracking the code on the Dead Sea Scrolls. He has worked at Apple since the 80s and could have retired a decade ago but chose not to.

For the cherry on top of the unpleasant cake, Uncle Timothy (thinks pronouns are for Leftist radicals only) is sprawled in a chair by the window, frenetically bouncing his knee. He is a man of extremes. After listening to one episode of the Joe Rogan podcast, he ditched his pot-smoking drum circle in Golden Gate Park and enrolled in the nearest police academy. Now, he's the most devoted officer the law has ever had. *Terrifying.* He's proudly wearing his cop uniform. *Waiting for some praise and recognition around here!!* What he doesn't realize is that most of the people on this floor, in particular, have not had the best experiences with the authorities. Being restrained, tasered, drugged, dragged, hauled away, dumped off. He might as well wear a target on his back.

Luckily, Ellie's beloved grandmother, Gigi (she/her, but totally open!), sits on the bed, wearing a faux vintage cheetah print coat that reeks of patchouli. Ellie huffs it in. *Thank the Goddess for Gigi.*

Uncle Timothy opens the forum. 'I'd be lying if I said this *isn't* where I expected to see you next.'

Ellie dryly replies. 'Ha ha ha.'

Her mom joins in. 'It looks like you've been eating.'

'Oh, great. Let's trigger my ED right off the bat.'

Sue doubles down. 'Try to stay focused on the positive. What sparks joy for you here? Name three things. Don't think, just say them.'

'Mom. I'm not one of your clients.'

Gigi gives her a squeeze, and Sue notices, responding with an eye roll, which Uncle Timothy takes as his cue to ramp up the weird vibes.

'What do I always tell you? The struggle is *good*. Only losers quit. Joe Rogan.'

Gigi lets her son know who's boss. 'I have an idea. Why don't you and Joe swap places with Ellie for a day? See how you boys like it?'

Pleased, Ellie tries to break the tension. 'Actually, I do have something I wanted to tell you all, while you're here, so I might as well-'

Uncle Timothy cuts her off, a habit he'll never break. 'Let me guess, you're really pregnant, not just pulling our leg?! Who's the dad? Let me guess that loser from high school?'

Sue immediately interjects. 'Let's not make *any* assumptions. The other parent might be a man *or* a woman *or* one of those in-between people.' She crosses her arms. 'Times certainly have changed.'

Ellie tries to keep her cool. 'NO, I'm not actually pregnant. *Obviously*. I just wanted to say the ayahuasca was a one-time thing. I don't usually do drugs like that.'

Uncle Timothy's eyes may get stuck in the back of his head. 'Yeah, sure, okay.'

He now takes a stand, literally by standing in the middle of the room, raising the level of awkwardness to new heights. He looks down as he readies himself for this moment that he's *clearly* rehearsed in the mirror.

'You know, it's all about diet, rest, and exercise. You gotta eat clean, find your optimal sleep level and workout once, maybe twice a day. That's the only thing that will make any difference. I actually brought you something, I think it will help a lot more than all *this…*' He reaches into his camouflage backpack, handing Ellie a bundle of bananas. 'One a day and you'll be back to normal, in no time. Well, as normal as *you* can be.'

Gigi responds so Ellie doesn't have to. 'Should we tell the head of the hospital about this cure you've found? Maybe they can give everyone here some fruit and clear the place out?'

Stan laughs in the corner. He doesn't really believe in any form of medicine. Steve Jobs didn't buckle to Western pharmaceuticals, and neither will he. Sue keeps the eye rolls coming from across the room.

Even though Ellie's parents' relationship would best be described as "bitter," her dad oddly formed a friendship with his ex-brother-in-law, Uncle Timothy. It's an odd pairing but they found one thing in common: their shared love for a pint (or a keg). Sue has *no* idea about this friendship between her sworn enemy and her brother, even though everyone else in the room does. Stan would like to keep it that way. So would Uncle Timothy. Gigi could care less and wishes all these adults acted a bit more like *adults*.

Ellie attempts to mitigate the tension. 'Why don't I put something on?'

Turning on the TV, Ellie's favorite movie is playing. *Superbad*. Except it's the sequence with dick after dick after dick drawing. Slightly uncomfy but they're all grown adults. *Right?*

Horrified, Uncle Timothy stares. 'I'm not into this. No homo.'

Gigi waves him off. 'I love this movie.'

He shoots her a judgmental look. 'I'm sure you do.'

Nothing can turn Sue's frown upside down as continued phallus after phallus projects across the screen. Gigi and Ellie are less than discreet with their squeezes and nudges, basking in joy, ready to explode with laughter. Nothing makes them laugh more than NOT being able to laugh.

Finally, Stan speaks. 'Maybe not the best choice…' He makes a cutting motion at his neck, telling Ellie to turn off the penis art. Her dad rarely tells her what to do, or gives her much attention of any kind, so she finds herself immediately flustered, using force to hit the OFF button on the remote repeatedly, until it flies out of her hand, hitting the wall, just as Maisie enters.

'What is going on in here?! CODE RED!'

Gigi immediately comes to her granddaughter's defense. 'No, no, she's not trying to hurt anyone, she didn't mean to do that, there were just too many eggplants on the screen.'

Maisie scans the room, trying to get a hold of the dynamics. *Good luck, no one can figure this out.* She turns to Ellie. 'I'll come back.'

Stan spots his out as he quickly approaches the end of the bed. 'I'm gonna take off. I have some meetings this afternoon. Do you need anything?'

Uncle Timothy holds up her pill cup. 'Just more of these.'

'Right. Okay, well, see ya later.' Stan gives Ellie a quick pat on the foot as he's leaving.

A soft voice comes from the corner.

'Bye Stan.' Always count on Sue to make things *weirder.* She then turns to her brother. 'Shall we head to the cafeteria?'

Ellie feels a wave of relief. 'Yeah, maybe that's a good idea. You guys go, I can't...leave this locked entry floor.'

Gigi pipes in. 'I'm going to stay a while longer.'

Uncle Timothy is already out the door when Sue turns back to leave her daughter with one last piece of advice.

'I know you won't listen to me, but check out my latest YouTube video, the one called "Emotional Wake-Up Call." I think you need it.'

9

Reclining in bed with a tray of half-eaten food, Ellie is watching (thoroughly enjoying) a re-run of *Laguna Beach*. Maybe she can try her hand at surfing? *If these teens can do it, certainly she could too.* Something physical might help her feel grounded again and reconnect her with the Earth. Her surfing fantasy is interrupted when the phone rings.

'Melanie Margaret is on the line for you.'

'Oh, I'm busy, I've actually got so much to do…' The line clicks. *Shit.*

'Hell-low?!?'

Ellie can feel the desperation through the phone. 'Hi Melanie, how are you?'

Her dad's (second) wife, Melanie Margaret (prefers no pronouns) grew up near Laguna Beach, ironically. A proud homegrown Orange County resident, she married Ellie's dad within ten days of his oceanfront home purchase. *Interesting timing.* She refers to Ellie as her husband's daughter, careful to separate their relations. Melanie's more interested in the property value included in her marriage contract than the (step) parenting aspect. She views Ellie as more of a disruption than a bonus. But she'd *never* let anyone else know that; image is *everything* where she's from.

'Oh, I'm fine, darling. The better question is: how are *you*?'

'Doing fantastic.'

'I'd beg to differ. Look, I heard what's going on and I'm just going to hope you'll listen to me, for once. You need to snap out of it—this is all CRAZY!'

'Everything's perfectly under control, but thanks for checking in.'

'Your father works so hard and the last thing we, I mean HE, needs is to be getting these emergency phone calls about your shenanigans. We were at the after party for my high school reunion at Linda Bushnell's house. She's married to the CEO of Ask Jeeves. Their house is 20,000 square feet. 20,000! But could we enjoy ourselves?! No! Instead, we had to drop everything for you and all your *crazy* antics, once again.'

'I'm so sorry, that sounds very tough. Almost as tough as the migrant families at the border who sleep in cages under foil blankets-'

Dial tone.

Normally, Ellie would just brush it off. But there's something about sitting in a hospital bed, as someone like *that* calls to "support" her, that lights a fire in her belly. She dials the phone and waits for her cue. *Beep.*

'Hi there Melanie, I think you lost service, the call ended so quickly. I wanted to let you know that I've actually lost *all* phone privileges, I'm far too demented to talk anymore, so this is my last phone call. Not *ever*, just while I'm here. Anyway, can you tell my dad I love him? Thanks, you're a doll! Kiss kiss!'

Just as Ellie puts down the phone, Maisie enters and hands her another, the one she's been desperate to check.

PETE: Can I come see you?

MOTHER: Your Aunt Sally tripped on her new doormat this evening while bringing in her dogs. She may have internal bleeding. Imagine if it was on the curb...

DAD: Cabo trip is canceled. Can't get a refund on boat rental.

Other than that, she has hundreds of messages from Austin who has sent her an overwhelming amount of memes, trying to be supportive, but it would take her all night just to catch up, so instead, she sends a few crying emojis in return.

Maisie breaks her concentration. 'You're really lucky to have so many people that check on you. Most folks don't have that.'

'Yeah, it's almost annoying, you know. Like, *leave me alone already*, I get it, you're obsessed with me.' As if on cue, one last text comes through:

GIGI: Thinking of you. All my love xoxoxo

10

In the middle of the night, Ellie gets a feeling that hits her once every blue moon. The one where she doesn't want to be alone because the memories pierce her attempts to drown them. It's very rare, but when it happens, she needs someone, anyone, to be with. Usually, this leads to sending a barrage of *You up?* texts, followed by a brief scan of the dating apps, finding the nearest beating heart in a one-mile radius. But under these circumstances, she can't send out a mating call. However, there are a few options less than a mile away, so she goes on a hunt to find one.

Peeking her head out into the hallway, she instantly spots the gentleman from group therapy. Quickly, she (silently) slides her way down the hall, before anyone can tell her to go back to bed. She's been loving their secret chats, so much so that she recently dubbed him Mr. Jones, after deciding she liked him so much, she'd love to make him her property one day and the nickname just...stuck.

Mr. Jones (he/him) doesn't see her approach, as he stares out the window, like he's in another world. He has attempted to die four times but was unsuccessful, which to him, made sense because his whole life has been a continued series of failures; one after the next, after the next, after the next. He won't talk about what happened, but he hasn't felt joy in months or maybe even years, that is, until the day Ellie noticed him. He doesn't like her (or *any* woman) that way. *Not everything is sexual.* It's more something about her, she makes him feel alive.

As Ellie settles in on the loveseat beside him, she silently offers him an edible, hidden in her bra. He thankfully takes it. The moon shines bright, filling the room with soft light; not too much but enough to illuminate what's hidden in the darkness.

Mr. Jones starts the conversation, for once. 'You know, I've looked at the stars almost every night, since I was a kid.'

'GET OUT. Me too!' In high school, Ellie used to sneak out and go wander the beach, staring up at the night sky and picking up trash along the way. Of course, her family always accused her of sneaking out to do drugs (which was accurate sometimes, but not *ALL* the time). They always assumed the worst, even when she tried her best.

Mr. Jones points to the sky. 'See the bright one? You know that's not actually a star, that's Venus?'

Ellie smiles, knowingly. 'I know. I love her. She's *my* North Star.'

Mr. Jones sighs. 'Sometimes I feel like I lost my North Star, a long time ago.'

Ellie takes a moment before she responds, allowing his words to sit between them. She's trying to be a better listener, not a fixer.

He continues. 'You know, you might think I'm crazy for this-'

'You're talking to the poster girl of insanity. Please, go on.'

'When there's something heavy on my heart, this is where I come. Not *here*, but to the moon and the stars. And I swear, if you slow down and still yourself, they have answers for you.'

'I believe that, and I would never moon-shame you. I mean, we're all just stardust walking around, it makes sense that our ancestors in the sky are guiding us.'

Mr. Jones smiles, patting Ellie on the hand. 'You're an old soul, you know that?'

From down the hall, footsteps echo. *Spotted.*

'Ellie! Get back to your room!'

In a (scream) whisper, she retorts. 'We were just practicing an eye meditation. It's consensual, I promise!'

Maisie approaches. 'I don't give a rat's ass what you're doing. You know girl, this is the last time I'm gonna warn you.'

'Meditation of the eyeballs is actually *very* therapeutic, I can teach you how to do it, if you'd like.'

For the first time in a long time, Mr. Jones finds laughter bursting from deep inside his belly, and it lasts for more than a few seconds. He didn't know he could still do that.

Maisie, on the other hand, does not see the humor. 'Ellie! Enough!'

Turning back to her hospital bestie, Ellie expresses her gratitude for their time together with prayer hands and a bow. 'We'll pick this up another time.' She pats his shoulder (a good touch) as she heads back to her room.

* * *

In her (hospital) bed, Ellie decides it's time to try her (new) friend's method. She sits where the moonlight can perfectly hit her face, closing her eyes, silently (and passionately), asking the question that's been on her mind since the moment she checked into this place.

Suddenly, she knows. Clearly, some part of her *does* want to be a mother. A rather big part, actually. And if she ever *does* find herself pregnant, by whatever means, maybe she'll really consider having the baby. I mean, she'll still fight like hell for the right to choose, but maybe she doesn't need to write motherhood off, just because she's terrified of turning into her own. Maybe being a mother wouldn't be a total disaster. She can really only go up from here, right?

11

It's a beautiful morning in the psych ward. The deer are drinking from the creek outside. New (fake) flowers from the Dollar Store adorn the tables. The sun shines through the window bars, shedding light beams on the walls. Oh, and Ellie finally gets to leave.

Chilling behind her closed bedroom door, she waits for Maisie, the only person in this place who can properly discharge her. It took her all of thirteen seconds to pack her (three) things. Just as her anxiety starts to perk up, she hears footsteps approaching (a skill she picked up in child-hood). But the door handle doesn't budge. Instead, an envelope slides underneath, flying across the floor.

A million thoughts race through Ellie's mind. *Who is this from? Is she in trouble? Does she have to stay longer?*

Before she can fall further down her thought rabbit hole, she slowly and carefully pulls the sealed envelope open, holding it gently, like it's made of rose petals. She closes her eyes, preparing herself for whatever bad news is coming next. Finally, she opens the page, letting the words sink into her soul.

Ellie,

I hate to break it to you, but there's nothing wrong with you. There's something wrong with the world.

You're one of the special ones. Don't let anybody tell you differently.

Keep shining,

Mr. Jones

Nothing has made her cry since she arrived here. Not being escorted to the hospital, or sleeping with a plastic doll, or being put through endless therapy. She's used to all that. Chaos, crisis, the rug being pulled out from under her feet. But the one thing she is very much *not* used to is someone seeing her for who she really is. She's spent her whole life being labeled as things to be hated: a whore, a queer, an anarchist, a floozy, a rebel, a loudmouth, and a wild, out-of-control weirdo. She hasn't taken it lying down, but she's built up an armor, to protect herself. Her walls keep out the bad and the only good she allows in is from those she trusts. Those who really see her. And so far, that's only been her grandmother and her forever best friend. *Two people.* Well, and her brother. *So, three.* That's it. The only thing in the world that makes her sob uncontrollably is someone being kind to her, out of the goodness of their heart, recognizing that she has a good heart too, despite what everyone else thinks.

First, it's just one tear, sliding from the corner of her eye. Then, she's face down in her pillow, releasing all the tears she's been holding, letting go so deeply that she doesn't even notice when another human appears at the door.

'Hey, sorry, I'll come back.'

Ellie quickly wipes her face, shoving the letter in her bag. 'No, yeah, no, it's okay. I was just thinking about all the baby sea turtles that won't make it to the water after they hatch. Did you know it's only one in a thousand who reach the ocean?'

Miserae knows she's lying. 'I just wanted to say goodbye. And give you this.' She hands Ellie the joint she left outside on her last "self-care" breakout.

'Jesus, where did you get this?'

'I wasn't creeping on you, I was down the creek a little, and I saw you left this and figured you'd want it. You know, now that you're free.'

'Thank you.' Ellie motions for Miserae to sit next to her on the bed.

They both lie back, looking at the ceiling. This is a new level of intimacy for Ellie, but she's tired and overwhelmed by all this thoughtfulness. Weird how she spent her whole life looking for real friends, only to find them in this place. For some reason, she feels like she can trust Miserae. So, she asks her something that's been on her mind.

'Do you ever wonder what you're doing here?'

'Like on Earth or here?'

'Both.'

'Every day.'

'Yeah, me too.'

Clomp. Clomp. Clomp. Footsteps charge down the hallway. Daniel is chasing another resident, pretending to have a fake taser. 'C'mere, or else I swear I'll zap ya with this!!'

Weirded out by the casual violence that has become so common here (and really, everywhere), Miserae takes this as her opportunity to ask Ellie her own existential question.

'Why are people the worst?'

Ellie smiles. 'There's always good people.'

Smiling back, Miserae dead pans straight into Ellie's eyes. 'There's always people that don't deserve to exist.'

The kinship radiates between them. Ellie bursts into laughter, feeling a little too exposed. *Baby steps.* Neither of them notices the new person at the door.

'HEY! Girls, off the bed! No funny business on my watch! Ellie, follow me.'

Ellie's been dreaming of this moment for weeks, and now, a part of her doesn't want to leave. Quickly, she gives Miserae a heartfelt good touch (a hug). To her, a hug is like a blessing for the body, and like Gloria said: If we bless our bodies, our bodies will bless us. Right now, Ellie could use some blessings.

Heading towards the door, she gets that feeling she (usually) only gets on vacation. *My body will never be in this room again. Or will it?*

Shaking it off and quickly stepping through the threshold towards the exit, her brain finally gives her a positive answer: *Hopefully, never again.*

part two:
the (almost) immaculate
conception

12

It feels like Ellie never left. Delighted to be back at her place, living amongst her things, she has developed a newfound sense of wonder and awe for the simplest elements of her apartment: her collage wall featuring Matisse, Hilma af Klint, and Picasso; her colored glass bottles; the wind chimes Gigi brought her from Peru; her plants (all named after planets: Jupiter, Pluto, Neptune, Your-anus); her oracle cards, sage, and crystals; and most importantly, her beautiful, comfortable bed, which she's not alone in.

Within approximately eight hours of being free, as if propelled by some unstoppable force, Ellie and Pete found themselves in a "check-in" exchange that quickly took a different energetic turn.

PETE: How are you feeling? Thinking of you and hoping all goes well.

Thank you! I'm feeling good, back to my old self. How are you?

PETE: Oh, you know, same old, same old. Good luck with everything, Ellie. I'm always here for you.

That last message gave her pause. Ellie hoped this formal facade would fade, now that she's "on the outside," as they say. Throughout her "vacation," Pete was constantly sending her letters, stuffed animals, and even managed to have the old school smut magazines she loves smuggled in. *Not for the perv factor, for the art of it all.* He did all that, even after everything. Her phone dings again.

PETE: I've really missed you.

I miss you too.

Within two seconds, there's a response.

PETE: Are you back yet?

Yes, sir. Released without bail today! Deciding what to do first...

This was not *entirely* true. Immediately upon her release, Ellie did multiple laps of all her favorite spots, everything she missed while she was "away." She went to town at Lemonade, ordering a full feast and even treating herself to the macarons, not counting one single calorie. She meditated at the Japanese Tea Garden, took new profile pictures at Crissy Field, and ran three laps of the entirety of Golden Gate Park, all in less than five hours. *Hypomania? Or just excitement to be free? A topic to discuss with Moseby.*

PETE: Can I see you?

I was going to ask the same thing.

PETE: Where are you?

My place. Come over.

Exactly seven minutes later, Pete arrives at her front door. *Record timing.*

In the words of The Killers, it starts off with a kiss. As he steps through her door, he embraces her and naturally, their lips met. Foreheads pressed together, they each pull back a little, until the other one goes in for it again. Until Pete moves down to her neck.

Pulling back, he looks in her eyes. 'Is this okay?'

Softly nodding, Ellie has never wanted anything more. As they fold into each other, all she can think is:

If this isn't sacred, then I don't know what is.

13

There's just two things Ellie has been putting off. *Two? Not bad!* The biggest one comes with that *familiar* feeling, with an emphasis on *family*. Unfortunately, her procrastination must come to a screeching halt. Fortunately, Gigi is at her side and they're at their favorite spot: the Palace of Fine Arts.

The designer of the Palace, Bernard Maybeck, wanted it to resemble a Roman ruin, symbolizing "the mortality of grandeur and the vanity of human wishes." Gigi always explained to Ellie that instead of looking at things as "ruins" to think of them as "reminders." That even though everything ends, there's still some use in having fun while it lasts.

Ever since Ellie was little, she's dreamt of living in this neighborhood—and her grandma fed those dreams. They'd walk around the Palace pond, imagining the future, admiring the various homes, and picking out their favorites. However, when Ellie's kindergarten class took a field trip to the Exploratorium (before it was relocated to Pier 39 - *shudder*), somehow, she snuck away, wandering through the Marina streets alone, looking for new real estate to show Gigi. This led to quite a bit of trouble, and her grandmother being labeled a "bad influence."

As an adult, Ellie still loves the Marina because it's where she first learned magical places exist. And as fate would have it, her grandma was the one who finally did find her a home here. An "old friend" who owned an adorable backhouse that his partner once used as an art studio, agreed to rent it at a rate that is unheard of in the entirety of the Bay Area. Only $800 per month to live in the cutest, pink stucco one bed, all within walking distance of the Presidio, Crissy Field, and of course, their favorite Palace.

Under the grand rotunda, Gigi heads towards the water to secretly feed the swans (against the multiple warning signs not to).

'How's your love life?'

'Fine.'

This is the other thing Ellie has been procrastinating on. She's been trying to be better with Pete since their night together. He couldn't be more loving, supportive, feminist, softly anarchist, and open-minded. And yet, there's nothing that scares her more than their connection.

Gigi gives her a look. 'You know my opinion.'

'Yes, I know, thank you. I'm still figuring it out. It's my journey.'

'Just don't wait too long. Have you had any fun lately?'

It's hard for her to lie to Gigi, so she simply omits her night of passion.

'I've been running around catching up on things. Getting my life back together.'

'Oh, honey. *That's* your issue. You need to *live* a little.'

'Last time I did that, it didn't go so well…if you recall.'

'Are you going to punish yourself forever?'

Ellie is silent, for once.

'It's all going to be okay, Grammy. You know that, right?'

Gigi calls her grandchildren Grammy, as a way of combating ageism.

'If you say so…'

They smile at each other, as the swans smile at them, waiting for more breadcrumbs to fall from Gigi's pocket.

14

When it's time to get into Bertha, Ellie reminds herself that she *does* actively support the battle against ageism. *Must work on expanding that belief to include Gigi's driving.* Even though she prefers cars with working seat belts, her grandmother loves this rundown VW Beetle that's seen better days. Ellie does a little energetic protection ritual for the three of them (Bertha included). Gigi has proven to be Ellie's ride or die protector, time and time again. If letting her sit in Bertha's driver's seat leans more towards the "die" edge of things, plunging through the hills with squeaky brakes, so be it.

To set the mood as the dynamic duo sputters their way across the city, Gigi has the Beatles cued up on full blast due to the hearing issues she *doesn't* have. Unlike the rest of the family, the only altar Gigi worships at is the one she created in her own home, for John, Paul, George, and Ringo (*no offense to Matthew, Mark, Luke, and John*). Her love language is sharing her favorite songs, which she does, often. Today she's chosen a classic. "Let It Be." *Fitting.*

Earlier this year, Ellie's family mutually decided to make a mass migration (*an exodus, really*) down to southern California as the country was "dividing." Their group text was filled with articles about how San Francisco is a hellscape and filled with "snowflakes." So, Ellie's freedom-loving relatives searched for a better life, finding refuge in the most elitist bubble in the country: Orange County. *But don't tell them that!* Her dad went first, the rest followed soon after: her mom, uncle, and even Austin's dad. Honestly, Ellie couldn't be happier. The Bay Area does feel lighter without them around. *Au revoir, famille!*

Ironically, even though Ellie's parents despise each other, neither of them would give up living in the best neighborhood in their (new) community of Laguna Beach. So, on opposite ends of the same street, her parents have done a superb job at creating division—in their family, with their (new) neighbors, and in their beachside community. They will both live on Victoria Drive, overlooking the ocean, and that's that. *Everyone else can pick a side!*

No matter where her parents go, there will always be a ravine between them. However, some of her family still kept roots in the Bay Area. Her dad didn't sell his condo in the city. A *modest* piece of real estate: a simple, quaint little 3 bed/3 bath penthouse in Pacific Heights, the neighborhood known for "Billionaire's Row." Ironically, many of Ellie's "clients" live in the same area, but most would pretend they don't recognize her, if ever confronted. Stan and Melanie picked up this little weekend escape pad when it was listed for just over 17 million dollars. His (second) wife *loves* to tell everyone the listing price, the square footage, and the net worth of all their neighbors.

Bertha finds a parking spot on Broderick (only the steepest hill in the whole neighborhood), while Ellie braces herself, for both the emergency brake and what's to come.

Making the death march up the stairs to the front buzzer, she finally admits her feelings to Gigi (the only person who ever gets to hear them).

'I'm feeling really tense.'

With a heavy dose of sarcasm, Gigi replies. 'Why ever would *that* be?'

These visits are always the *opposite* of fun. But with Gigi in tow, it'll make things funn*ier*, at least. Ellie hopes their matrilineal ESP connection will come in handy today. *She certainly needs it.*

The front door is ajar, and a fluffy dog comes running up to greet them, putting its head directly into Ellie's crotch. Gigi melts with laughter, as Ellie looks at the collar to find the dog's name. She immediately gestures to Gigi to take a look, which only pours gasoline on the laughing fit. *This is going to be interesting.*

* * *

'New York was fabulous. But get this, our breakfast cost two hundred and fifty dollars one day. Can you believe it?'

Table conversation is always a treat. Melanie Margaret leads and everyone else swallows it down, both the chat and the food. Her favorite topic of late is the cost of everything. She loves to pretend to be a "bargain hunter" while living on Stan's (luxurious) dimes.

She continues. 'Your father and I, we just went over to Brooklyn, because I'm not going to pay hundreds of dollars for breakfast!!'

Gigi politely responds, focusing on cutting her food to keep her poise. 'That sounds extremely rough. Almost as rough as the 20% of school children who don't get breakfast every morning. Or the 690 million people around the world who are starving and undernourished.'

Ellie - and even her dad - can't help but softly smile into their plates. Complaining about the cost of food on vacation while sitting in a luxury home is…*something*.

Melanie is not pleased. 'We all know who you voted for, you don't need to advertise it.'

Stan tries to maintain homeostasis. 'No politics at the table.'

Offended that her engaging story about breakfast prices in Manhattan has been interrupted, Melanie reroutes the conversation, focusing on her usual victim. Her husband's daughter.

'I see you RSVP'd to the gala with a plus one. Who will you be bringing?'

'Oh, just Austin.'

'Hmmph. I was hoping you'd met a nice fella.'

Stan shoots her a look. 'Lay off it.'

Melanie fires back. 'Well, it will be impossible to meet a husband if you're always with…him. Or is it *her* now?'

Ellie breaks in. 'Yeah, we like to travel as a pair and we basically do everything together. Except go to the bathroom.' *Awkward.*

'I always thought you two would get married. Maybe there's still a chance, you just never know.'

Gigi chomps at this opportunity. 'Or maybe *your* son will end up with Austin. Love always finds a way.'

Melanie has an (estranged) son from her first marriage. A topic to *never* be discussed. Everyone stares at their plate like they've never seen a meal before. The only being in the room who isn't feeling the tension is the dog, who's begging for a bite.

Ellie takes the bait, sneaking the dog a crouton. 'How'd you come up with the name for her? Nellie, is it?'

Gigi almost chokes on the halibut as Stan tenses up, like a slinky that just desperately wants to be released down a flight of stairs.

Melanie turns to Ellie, smug as hell. 'You know how I am with names. I'm great with them. This one just came to me one day.'

With a genuine smile, Gigi replies. 'Oh, it's *really* cute. Catchy. And kinda familiar…'

Melanie turns her attention to the being she respects the most, her new "rescue" dog (a.k.a. the pure bred $3,000 animal she "saved" from a house in Utah). Calling out to her pet, for the first time, her voice carries a hint of love. 'Nellie, you're a good girl. I'll get you your fish in a minute.'

Stan pauses. 'Oh, uh, I gave the halibut to Gigi.'

Melanie turns back to her dog, about to combust with nerves. 'I'm so, so sorry, my sweet Nellie Boo Bear. If I'd known, I wouldn't have let everyone here just eat your dinner like that.'

Stan is now getting pissed. 'We can order more.'

Melanie holds up a "cease and desist" hand. Scooting back from the table, she marches to the (servant's) kitchen, only to come back seconds later, holding a birthday cake and a butcher knife. A very *So I Married an Axe Murderer* vibe. She thrusts it in Ellie's direction, oddly blade first.

'Here, why don't *you* cut the cake for your father's birthday?!' With that, she stomps out of the room, with Nellie at her heels.

Gigi attempts to lighten the mood. 'Are you even allowed to hold sharp objects?'

Ellie plays along. 'Not exactly…who wants the first piece?'

With that, Stan goes on a hunt to find his (second) wife in one of their many rooms with wainscoted walls. *Lord help him.* So, the dynamic duo take to the drawing room, sipping the last of the wine, staring at the grand piano, not saying a word. The silence is golden.

Ellie knows they're both having the same memory, being around this piano. The last time she sat on that piano bench was with her grandfather, Gigi's husband. Ellie will never forget the smile on her grandpa's face, beaming at her while they played *When the Saints Go Marching In* together. Of course, her grandfather left her the piano in his will, but since she was only nine, it ended up in her parent's living room. By the time they divorced, it became one more object to fight over, and somehow, her dad ended up with it. But her mom is currently in a battle to get it back. Neither of them will ever pause to remember it was actually meant for *her*.

But seeing it, here and now, all Ellie can think of is the sweetness, and she knows that's what Gigi's thinking about too. The kindness and softness and gentleness of her grandfather. A man who took the time to teach her piano (even when she forgot to practice). Who found so much joy in making music and singing (even when he was mostly off-key). He kept a tip cup on the edge, filled with coins, and somehow, it's still there. His legacy of goodness survived the bitterness between her parents. *Maybe it still lives in her, too?* Her reverie suddenly ends when a napkin lands in her lap.

'It's been twenty minutes; I think our time here is up.'

Gigi is right. What's the point in staying? Like a fire drill in a Chicago winter, they rush towards the exit, getting their shoes on as quickly as possible. Just as Ellie has her hand on the doorknob, she hears the footsteps coming down the hall.

'I'll tell your father you couldn't stay.' Melanie moves between Ellie and the door, blocking the dynamic duo's exit. 'And I'll pray for you.'

'Oh, you don't need to do that.'

'Oh, but I do.'

'Oh, but you don't.'

'Oh, but I will.'

15

'Can we make a quick stop on the way home?' Gigi gives Ellie that guilty until proven innocent look. *Uh oh. She's up to something.*

Ellie nods in agreement, knowing she doesn't really have much of a choice. When Gigi sets her mind to something, it happens. At the stoplight at the Embarcadero, the moment the light turns green, Bertha makes a sharp right (a little too sharp), instead of a left. *Oh brother. They're headed to the Bay Bridge. To Gigi's stomping grounds.*

Gigi is a local celebrity in Berkeley—and honestly, she loves it. Fame suits her like a mink coat. *Vintage, of course. Cool it, PETA.* She has been a staple at every protest, sit-in, and free love fest in the Bay Area since the 60s. The entryway to her bungalow is filled with framed photos of her hugging the Beatles. Rumor has it one of her children is George's love child—but Ellie finds this nearly impossible to believe. Certainly not her mother or Uncle Timothy. *Aunt Sally, maybe?*

Outside of the Beatles memorabilia and tokens from past lovers, Gigi's home is also filled with roses, both inside and out. Her blooming bushes have been featured in the local magazines, and she keeps fresh-cut vases filled to the brim in every room (and on every flat surface area). Even though Gigi could make millions on the sale of her home, she has refused to cash in on her well-placed bungalow, holding out against The Man. Of course, her children have their eye on it (as well as her property in Tahoe), banking on a hefty inheritance, but little do they know that hippie dippy Gigi has left a detailed estate plan, which mandates the bungalow *not* be sold. *Revenge is best served in legal writing.*

Gigi motions for Ellie to take a seat on the rose upholstered couch, as she opens the windows, and lights the incense, along with her votive candle to John. She honors a different Beatle each week; even though Paul and Ringo are still alive, she feels they're connected to her on a soul family level.

A loud knock at the door breaks the silence. Ellie panics. 'Who did you invite here? I'm really not up for more company, that dinner was a lot.'

'Relax, Grammy. It is time.'

Swinging open the door, Gigi greets her friend Suzie (currently known as Earth Feather) with a kiss on both cheeks. Earth Feather is carrying a large doctor's bag. *Vintage, of course.*

Ellie starts wringing her hands. 'Gigi, look, I told you that I'll give you whatever organs you need, and we can stockpile blood for the apocalypse, but I don't think right now is a good time.'

Earth Feather sits down next to Ellie, holding both her shoulders. 'Oh, you're magic, sweetie. I can see the purple in your aura.'

Ellie blushes, grateful for any compliment on her appearance, even the energetic parts she can't see. 'Thank you, I've been doing a lot of ASMR meditations before bed and I think it's really-'

'The hour is almost near!' Gigi gestures towards the clock, which is on the verge of striking nine.

'Is there a new show on? Or is this another cleansing ritual?'

Earth Feather and Gigi exchange a knowing glance. 'More of a sacred *marking* ritual.'

Ellie gulps, feeling both excited and nervous. She knew this day was coming and there's no escaping it now. She promised Gigi they could get matching tattoos *and* that Gigi could pick the design and placement. *Let's just hope it's not head-to-toe body art. You never know with Gigi.*

But if there's anyone she trusts in this dimension, it's her grandmother. And therefore, by default, Earth Feather too.

16

Not much about Ellie's life has really changed since her "vacation," except the overall vibe just feels… different. However, work is still pretty much the same, as not much *ever* changes there. Men have been paying women for their "services" for centuries. Nothing revolutionary about that.

For once in her life, she's excited to be heading back. Being "away" for so long forced her to see that she actually derives quite a bit of her self-worth from her ability to make money. *A product of capitalism, yes, and another topic for Moseby, most definitely.* But still, a source of self-esteem. *Something she needs a boost of, stat.*

Ellie speeds through her work prep routine. Pasties, lacy crop top, eyeliner, post-its, pregnancy test, pigtails, glitter, stilettos, and *Lady Jane* jacket. She pounds two glasses of water, tosses the test in the trash without a second glance (it's always negative), and done. The pregnancy test is honestly a waste of plastic, not that anyone around here would care about that. *Speak of the devil.*

Jake screams through the locker room door. 'Welcome back honey.'

At least her boss is being nicer. *For now.*

* * *

Waiting in the wings in only a thong and heels, Ellie loses herself in deep contemplation about her life (mostly to distract herself from her stage fright). She thought this job would make her hate men, but ironically, it's done the opposite. She feels sorry for them. Even though most people would never believe her, Ellie knows she's providing a greater service to the world. She's consoled CEOs, founders, venture capitalists, telling them it will all be okay, repeating lines from her therapist, all while wishing society would just normalize therapy for men. Men are taught to hold in their emotions, to never cry, and to suck it up. Most don't seek help and they don't know how to unpack their traumas—but those feelings still exist and they overflow into their daily lives, until they end up at a strip club, crying in one of the private rooms, begging to be held by a young woman in a G-string. Essentially, she's offering mental health support to the most successful men in San Francisco, and therefore, the planet. *If that's not fulfilling one's purpose, then what is?!*

The cheugy announcer gets on the mic, way too proud of the power he holds in this place.

'And now, please welcome to the stage, our House Favorite, back from vacation, the one, the only, the juicy, LADY JANE!'

Ellie makes a cringe face as she walks onto the stage, dodging Jake's second attempt at giving her a hug. Her dancing effort is at roughly five percent—and honestly, that's fine. It doesn't matter because the customers are only here to stare at her. She could lie down and take a nap and they'd still watch. *And probably pay her for it!*

She does various dances, not really sexual, and starts goading the crowd to open their wallets. Per usual, she's able to get a wad of cash just by pantomiming the action. A pair of knockers can make even the smartest bro dumb.

She's feeling herself starting to get her groove back. *Even having fun?* That is, until a group of guys, around her age, walk in. *Oh fuck.*

Other dancers join her on stage and Jake motions for her to move to the front. She pretends not to see him until he makes it glaringly obvious, threatening her with more forced affection. Hesitantly, she moves forward, trying to keep her face hidden.

Of course, the pack of guys sit right in front of her. She slowly dances their way, reluctant but also with a wave of newfound confidence.

Douchebag #1 speaks first, as expected. 'Well, look who it is.'

Slyly, Ellie refuses to let him get the best of her. 'I'm sorry, do I know you?'

Incoming: Douchebag #2. 'Oh that's rich, Ellie. Look at you, all grown up.'

They all sit back in their chairs, except for one, who looks concerned. Adam. The one who threw a party at her mom's old house and then called her a slut. She's known this "wolf" pack for most of her life—knows what streets their parents live on, who had a letter jacket, and which ones hooked up with Austin behind closed doors. Most of them were handed an SVP title straight out of school, inheriting access to a trust fund and leveraging their parent's connections. She knew they'd eventually all cross paths. San Francisco *is* a small city.

Weirdly, Pete ran into a few of them while she was "away." He works for the government, doing a job he can never tell anyone about. Sometimes, Ellie wonders if the whole "secret government job" is a lie. But Pete isn't like that. She just wishes she could be more like him. Sometimes it feels like her lies have a mind of their own. Flying out of her mouth before she can catch them. When Pete told her how he met with this group of "gentlemen" for "work," all she could think was: *What business does the government have with these big banks and tech companies?! What could they possibly be negotiating, in private?* She doesn't want to know. *Sometimes, ignorance is necessary. For her mental health.*

Douchebag #1 wants to show off, pompously spreading his legs. 'Saddle up, Ellie.'

'My name is Lady.'

#2 fluffs his feathers a bit, peacocking hard. 'Sure it is. You don't look like a lady to me, you look like a...'

Daring him, Ellie responds. 'Like a *what?*'

Then, Adam, the concerned, "nice" guy, the only one whose name she remembers, steps in. 'Hey, hey, let's all take it easy. How much for a private?'

Ellie is beyond confused. *Why is he doing this?*

* * *

Back in her least favorite private room, Ellie sits perpendicular to her former nemesis. 'Well, I guess, thank you for...that.'

'Look, I'm sorry about those guys, they can be real dicks.'

'Nothing I haven't seen before.'

'Yeah, I'm sure. I mean, I didn't mean it like that. God, sorry.'

'It's okay. So, do you work around here? It's been forever since I've seen you.'

'Yeah, it has been a long time.' Adam unzips his puffer vest, letting his shoulders down a bit. 'I'm right down the street actually. Near City Hall.' Running his fingers through his hair, his tone swiftly changes. 'Ellie, why are you working here? Do you need a loan or something?'

Pretending not to hear his (rather rude) question, she notices how nervous he seems. Like *really* nervous. There's something odd going on here. *Does she smell or something?*

But just like that, the memory drops in, like an avalanche. *Of course, he's shitting his pants. He should be.*

Ellie lets the silence fill the room, like smoke, before she finally speaks.

'Actually, I *do* remember the last time I saw you and your buddies out there.'

She ran into them at a house party in Berkeley after high school. It was right before she met Pete. She was overserved—and those guys locked her in a bathroom. She can still feel what her body remembered but her brain forgot: squirming away, trying to say no, while coming in and out of consciousness. They poured water on her white shirt, groped her, and lord knows what else, until Austin saved her. She can still hear their laughs, each and every one.

Recognition sets over Adam's face. 'Look, I don't want this to turn into a #MeToo thing. You don't really have a case and from what I recall, it was consensual. Heck, you were practically begging for it, the way you were dressed. To be clear, there's no money in this for you. I can give you a loan separately, you know, to get you out of this sex work you're doing, but you'll have to sign an agreement, promising to keep the past in the past. Plus, I'm doing the right thing *now*, so yeah.'

As he gets up to leave, Ellie steps in front of him, putting a hand up to block his way. 'I know this might be something you don't hear very often so listen closely…' She leans in and whispers in his ear. 'If anyone ever says this to you, I hope you fucking listen the next time. Are you ready for it? Here's the magic word: No. No, you scumbag piece of shit.'

Adam's jaw drops, aghast that someone *like her* would have the nerve to talk to someone *like him* like that. 'They told me you were crazy.'

Ellie composes herself as she walks out the door, giving the signal to security to escort him out. Sure, it's not *all* men who are terrible, but the ones who are, they cause so much damage and havoc, not only in strip clubs, but for centuries, everywhere in the world. Men like that, they dominate, manipulate, abuse, conquer, rape, take, and feel entitled to it. They twist reality, make things distorted, and can't understand a universe where they're *equal* to anyone. Because they're so used to living life on top, to being able to do whatever the fuck they want, whenever they want. *It's exhausting.*

As she gets back on stage, watching this leech from her past be led towards the exit, she feels something hard hit her back. And then it happens again. And again and again and again. *Like she's getting stoned, not in a good way.*

Coins. The other guys are throwing metal money at her. And it hurts. Luckily, she does something her younger self wanted to do, but wasn't able to. She asks for help, letting security pounce on this pack of rats— and then, she leaves.

She walks the fuck away.

<h1 style="text-align:center">17</h1>

The best thing about Jones family parties is the shared, unspoken yet firmly palpable feeling in the air, that no one, not one single soul, wants to be there. For once, all Ellie wants to do is blend in. But with pink hair and fishnet tights, she stands out wherever she goes, especially at her mother's house. She's been dreading this day for weeks, while the rest of her family has been *living* for this moment, all year.

Moseby has been working with her on staying in the present. *But what if the present sucks?* Ellie tries to focus on the celebration ahead: the "Freedom" BBQ, hosted as her mom's "last hurrah" in Belvedere, to celebrate the day this country became "free." *Sure. For everyone but queers, women, and ANY person of color, not to mention the Native Americans!!!*

Even though Ellie and Austin escaped across the Bay, the one thing they didn't factor in was that the water wouldn't protect them from having to return. After all, there were bridges. Famous ones, at that. They'd both built a suspension bridge of disbelief in their minds, forgetting that the pathway leading to their freedom would also be their gateway to return. Neither of them liked the feeling when they had to do the latter. Luckily, this is their last journey in this direction (North) for a while, as the entire family will (officially) become permanent residents of Orange County by the end of the summer. *Hallelujah!*

As the besties reluctantly drive over the Golden Gate, Austin tries to lighten the mood. Always prepared for everything, they ask, 'Did you bring earmuffs?'

Ellie pulls out the most ridiculous looking pair possible, with rainbows and skulls and glitter. 'Yeah, I only had these ones from the Heavy Petting Zoo at Burning Man.'

'Loves it. Why exactly do we need ear protection again? I thought fireworks were illegal.'

'Oh, it's better than that. Just you wait and see.'

'I don't like surprises with your family, they never end well.'

Ellie basks in the comfort of the light sparkling off the Bay, closing her eyes, looking from the water to the sun, embracing the last minutes of peace before the mayhem. As the car races towards the rainbow-lined Robin Williams Tunnel, she finds herself bracing for impact.

* * *

Bang. Bang. Bang. Ellie cannot believe her eyes (or her covered ears). This is a new low, even for her family. Things couldn't be worse. The cops arrived, and of course, everyone was over-the-moon delighted. The squad cars pulled up, sirens and lights blaring, eager to watch the post-BBQ surprise that Ellie's uncle planned. A gun salute, straight into the Belvedere Lagoon.

With every shot fired, Ellie can't help but wince and Austin looks like they are being physically operated on with no anesthetic. Somewhere during this hellish experience, they made their way to hit the punch bowl, but Ellie is (newly) attempting to be sober in alignment with her new practice of mindfulness—a.k.a. staying in the moment. Truthfully, all she wants is to teleport to anywhere but here. Meanwhile, Gigi is openly smoking a cig, as a one-woman protest. She quit smoking over thirty years ago, but she lets herself go wild on what she calls "the most colonial day of the year."

As the bullets hit the water, this trio has the same thoughts rushing through their heads, telepathically communicating to one another with their eyes. *What if a baby seal eats a bullet? How are the cops supporting this? When can we get the bloody hell out of here?*

Of course, Uncle Timothy planned this literal gun show, all by himself. He prides himself on starting the only "Freedom Ferry" in California, one that allows for open carry of all weapons. The County of San Francisco is currently in litigation, desperately trying to change the maritime laws, so he'll be sailing the boat down to Orange County, where it will be welcomed with open arms (literally).

Today is his last Bay Area show and he wants to make it *extra* special. On the back lawn of his sister's recently "In Escrow" Belvedere home, overlooking the water, he set up a full folding table with 18 different types of firearms and had the Freedom Ferry dock right in the lagoon.

65

Of course, during the demonstration, he's been very careful not to shoot too closely to his cherished vessel. He's only made it through exhibiting three weapons so far, taking his sweet time to hold, caress, and show off each new "piece" to his audience of admirers. His girlfriend Sandra (she/her, if she must) couldn't be less interested. She asked for a boob job on her 13th birthday and actually got it—something Ellie's uncle loves to brag about to his buddies at the station: his girlfriend's "flawless" body.

Today, she's not too happy to be in charge of Little Timmy (TBD), her significant other's son, from his first marriage. Even she thinks this whole gun show is ridiculous. *Little Timmy needs sleep, not a blown-out eardrum.*

Noticing her daughter's displeasure with the flying bullets, Sue gestures to Ellie to smile. If she could, her mom would tattoo a smiley face over Ellie's actual face.

Meanwhile, Austin's dad, Ray (also refuses to declare), is scoffing at the two besties, clearly intoxicated with liquid courage. He's an Evangelical preacher. *Enough said.* He is absolutely worshiped at his megachurch, so it's utterly *shocking* to him when his own child doesn't revere him in the same way everyone else does. *Like a God.* But Ray does have one thing in common with his spawn: he's also closeted. *At the moment.* Ray absolutely hates when Austin acts in any way feminine. Like right now, screeching and hiding from the "celebratory" gunshots. He wants Austin to stand "like a man" and admire the bullets "like a goddamn American."

Finally, Uncle Timothy puts his last gun down, turning to the crowd. 'Thank you for coming, I didn't think so many of you would show up like this. Don't forget to tag me, my handle is CaliGunBoat. You know, I'd like us to take a moment today, to honor not just this holiday, but also, our freedom. I am so goddamn proud to be a rifle owner, a handgun owner, a pistol owner, I mean, I could go on for days. But now, I'd like to open up the floor to anyone else who'd like to say something they love about this beautiful country we are so lucky to live in. All this empty land, our ancestors just found and settled, finally building a better future for us and allowing us to be here, now, with our guns.'

The cops are filming him, even Live streaming, to show off this delightful patriotic celebration.

Austin whispers to Ellie. 'This is *so* problematic, it will *definitely* go viral.'

Ellie looks at them, locking eyes with Gigi too, as she takes a metaphoric leap onto the plank, putting one foot in front of the other, approaching her uncle, participating in the gun show she swore to never enter, like a liberal pirate.

Finally, she speaks. 'I actually have a few words I'd like to say.'

Attempting to cut her off, her high-strung mother jumps in. 'Elizabeth, this is not the time for your politics.'

Shocked, the "fearless" Uncle Timothy stands back, for once allowing his niece to have the spotlight. Austin and Gigi are currently on the verge of fainting, they are so horrified by what Ellie's doing, wondering why she would *ever* subject herself to this.

'It's not political, Mom. Although Gloria Steinem did say politics *are* personal, or maybe it was the other way around. Regardless, I'm not trying to preach. I have something I need to tell you all, so I'll make it quick.'

No one utters a word.

'Okay, well, first, I'm single.' A few of the cops perk up in the background. 'But I'm not available. To men. At the moment. Um, I broke up with Pete, who most of you know, and I met someone new. Her name is Bethlehem and we met in spin class. She's from New Jersey, so, yeah, basically, I'm dating her now but it's still early days.'

With that, she simply walks off the plank, back towards her (two) supporters, with all eyes on her. Gigi and Austin are (silently) cheering like they just received a jackpot of beads at Mardi Gras, but Sue quickly shushes them before addressing the partygoers.

'Oh, our Ellie, she's always one to share too much. Honey, this is just a phase, you don't need to announce it to the whole neighborhood! We all know you live in San Francisco! Plus, what about the grandchildren you owe me?'

Some laughs break up a bit of the tension, lingering in the air along with the leftover gun smoke. Looking at the ground, Uncle Timothy sidles back up to the center, holding his chin while openly smirking.

'Well, I wish I could say I was surprised but I saw this one coming from a mile away. I've always known you were a queer, well before you did. Are you the man or the woman in your new relationship, with what was her name? Nazareth? Oh, sorry, I mean, Bethlehem?'

Ellie straightens up, ready to finally take on her uncle. She might not be able to say anything about the guns, but she can certainly stand up for the girls and the gays.

'Actually, her name is Bethlehem. She was raised in the foster system, got a scholarship to UCSF, studied biochemistry, and is now a doctor, for your information. I know this will come as a complete shock, but not everything centers around "the man." Sometimes there is no man. Can you believe it?'

Austin comes up behind her, rubbing her shoulders, as a sign of support and also, a reminder to cool it. This is a battle she will never, ever win.

Uncle Timothy can't hide his grin. It's like he was waiting for her to get mad, even the slightest bit, so he could double down. 'You know, if you're gonna be a lesbian, you're gonna have to toughen up a bit, not get flustered so easily. Isn't that how you people are? What do they call it, butch?'

Shocked but not shocked, Ellie listens as (mostly) everyone has a good (homophobic) laugh, at her expense, per usual. This quickly triggers a break in her sober streak. *Sorry Moseby, but fuck presence.* She hits the punch bowl. And Gigi's joint. And her stash of edibles.

By the time the night is over, she doesn't even remember how much Uncle Timothy didn't stop making fun of her, while her mother kept commenting that it's all 'just a phase.'

At least Ellie finally told the truth. For once.

18

To distract herself (and avoid her emotions), Ellie starts watching YouTube videos made by anyone but her mom. Especially ones by landscape painters and illustrators. Inspired, she decides to make her own art, creating a collage of pictures…of her and Pete. *Not a good sign.*

Fifteen minutes later, she's burning said collage in her sink, for no particular reason other than she was once told that the key to manifesting is releasing.

From there, she hastily stomps towards the Presidio, taking deep inhales, bringing that eucalyptus scent deep into her second chakra. With every step, she pounds each foot, hoping the ground beneath her will absorb the confusion, the frustration, the sadness, the loneliness. All the feelings that come up when she thinks about her life. *The fear.*

Instead, she knows just what to do. When in doubt, head to the group chat.

~bEsTiEs~

I need to go out.

An instant response:

ROSA: Welcome back, girl. Let's party.

* * *

Across the bar, a dark-haired beauty keeps making eye contact with Ellie. *Is this a friends vibe? No, this is definitely more than a friends vibe.* Just as Ellie gets up to approach her, a burly guy scooches into her booth, blocking her path. *Great. Another disruption by a man! At least this one is cute.*

Awkwardly, she turns to face this eager stranger as he shoves his hand out.

'Hi, I'm Guy.'

Sarcastically, she sticks out her hand just as obnoxiously because when she's actually attracted to someone, she can't help but torment them.

'Hi, I'm Girl.'

'No, uh, my name really is Guy.'

'Does that work on all the ladies?'

He pulls out a business card, showing her:

Mama's Little Guy's Cookies
Guy Parker (he/they)
Owner

'Is that a new app or something? Or do you really make cookies with your mom?' *Why is she being so mean?!? He's really hot. Shit!*

'Cookies all the way, girl. Just like mama taught me. She's dead now, so you can feel like a dick now or later, your pick. But it's her recipe. Here, wait a second.'

As he's digging through his pockets, Ellie stares at him, enraptured. Until Rosa taps her on the shoulder, nodding towards the bathroom.

✳ ✳ ✳

The only reason Ellie and her friends come to The Mint, out of all the hot spots in the Castro, is because it's the one place they won't be recognized by anyone from work. *Usually.* To be honest, Gigi has been sneaking Ellie into this karaoke bar since she was eleven, swearing it's the "secret gem of San Francisco." But Rosa and Stacey would beg to differ, mostly *because of* the karaoke. They'd rather be at the Sugar Lounge, looking for more sugar daddies, although Rosa already has plenty of those.

As they each touch up their eyeliner and lipstick in the mirror, Ellie steers the conversation away from herself. 'How's the new guy?'

Rosa rolls her eyes. 'He's whatever. I get paid every Friday so you know.' She pauses, turning to Ellie. 'Girl, we've missed you.'

Okay, we're doing this. 'I missed you too.'

Cue Stacey. 'How are you doing with like…?'

Rosa is suddenly sympathetic. 'Yeah, we wanted to come visit but we weren't sure if we should.'

'No worries, it's all good, really. I'm sorry again about…what happened and everything.'

Stacey and Rosa don't say anything, hoping she'll open up more, but Ellie isn't in the mood for that.

'Well, I don't want to ruin the vibe. Let's just forget about it and have some fun.'

Stacey instantly replies. 'What's going on with you and Pete though? Are you guys still, like, a thing?'

'It's…complicated. I'm currently in the midst of a personal rebrand, trying to make this my hot girl summer. Or whatever they call it.'

Stacey softly takes Ellie's hands. 'Just never forget, I'm always here for you.'

Right.

* * *

'There you are! You have to try this.'

There he is. *Her antidote.*

Guy discreetly passes along a baggie full of cookies, like he's smuggling drugs at a Catholic high school—an immediate cue to Stacey and Rosa to walk away. He sees the skepticism on Ellie's face.

'I promise, they're clean. This is mama's recipe.'

Ellie looks at him, then looks at her friends, who should be *way* more concerned about her intaking *any* kind of substance after the last incident. As she slowly takes a gentle (yet seductive) bite, her brain fills with so many thoughts. *How is this guy, Guy, making a living from baked flour? In the Bay Area, of all places?! Most people here won't even eat gluten, let alone sugar!*

What she doesn't know (yet) is that after a massive corporate layoff plus the passing of his mother, Guy started a bakery, against the advice of everyone in his life. But he's been laughing all the way to the bank since, so the haters can literally eat it. He'll happily send them a sample, actually. His work life is so busy that he's not really looking for anything serious—but Ellie is one of the only femmes he's found himself attracted to in a hot minute.

'This is fucking delicious.'

All it took was one cookie and she was sold. If her and Guy start dating, she could refer to him as "my guy, Guy" and *that* would be really cute. And Insta grid-worthy.

The next thought that crosses Ellie's mind is how she wants to tell her brother about this: meeting a handsome cookie dude at The Mint, like something straight out of a rom-com. *Or a cheesy porn.* But instead, she wipes the thought from her brain *No. Not now.* Just as suddenly, Guy makes a sharp left.

'You have to do a song with me.'

'No, no, I'm alright, I don't like to be on stage.' She glances around the bar, daring her friends to say something. Unsurprisingly, they're nowhere to be found.

Guy playfully pokes her arm. 'I won't take no for an answer.'

'Well, that is what I like to call a Giant Red Flag.'

'Not like that, silly.'

Predictably, she takes Guy home, like a goodie bag from a birthday party. As soon as they arrive at her place, she remembers how much she hates when new people see her belongings. *Things reveal too much about a person's insides. What did she even leave out?*

'Oh, you live that sage life?'

Guy picks up her sage stick (homegrown), waving it around like a baton. She nabs it from his hands, like the final play at the Super Bowl.

'Yeah, I mean, I'm not like a Haight Ashbury hippie or anything, I just like to cleanse my plant's auras. It's really for *them*, not for me.'

'No, yeah, it's cool, I'm into it.'

He definitely thinks she's a freak. Great. But she really might have manifested him?! It'll only be a few more seconds before he spots the oracle cards. *Fuck.*

But instead, he focuses on her. 'So, what's your deal again? Tell me, how are you single?'

She feels the tension release a bit from her body, as she hands him water and also, takes a swift pull from hers.

'How much time do you have?'

'Remember what I told you before?'

Ellie searches through her mental archives of the night. *Oh yeah.* When they were singing on stage, he clearly mouthed 'I LIKE YOU' over the music. *Oh yeah, that.*

She tries to play it cool and does what she does best. Diverts the attention. 'I thought you liked Rosa…'

Guy adamantly shakes his head. 'Nah. I find you very attractive. Do you think I'm attractive?'

Ellie smiles at him, slyly. *Say less, my Guy.*

19

The next morning, somehow, she doesn't want to jump out of her skin. She has no grand delusions of going to brunch with him or even exchanging numbers. Although, there is always the option to slide into the DMs—but she'll leave that to him. For whatever reason, she's soothed by the fact that he'll probably ghost her, disappear into the San Francisco ether—and she can too.

And the sex. That's not the kind of sex you have with someone you want to date forever. It was...wild. Astronomical. Crazy, in a good way. And they both not only enjoyed it but completed it. Multiple times. She feels like a fully expressed, sexually liberated human. *Gloria Steinem would be so proud.*

Guy notices she's awake. 'Well, I think last night was fun, no?'

'I feel bad, you did most of the work, I was like a pillow princess and I shou-'

Luckily, he stops her while she's ahead. 'I enjoyed myself, did you?' *God, he really is woke as hell.*

'That thing you did...' *Is she blushing? What's happening to her?*

'You liked that?'

'I like you.'

The second the words leave her mouth, she wants to pull them back in. *Where did that come from? NO, NO, NO, NO, NO!* She wants to die, melt into the floor, be kidnapped by aliens, anything!

'Ahhhhh I like you too. And this is probably a good time to talk about that.'

Once again, she finds herself throwing back the covers to pop out of bed. 'No no no no no, please, we don't have to do this. I get it, trust me. I just meant, I like your *dick*. Not you. That's what I *meant* to say.'

Guy falls backwards onto the pillows, laughing. 'Girl, you are something else. Hey, do you wanna get breakfast? I know this great farm-to-table place, it's only a 10-minute walk and no one knows about it yet. It's quiet, all the food is grown right there in a garden, and it's not overrun by tourists or the Pacific Heights crowd. They'd never be caught dead that close to Dogpatch. No lines.'

As tempting as that offer sounds to her stomach, she must put an end to this. *Immediately.* This cannot be happening. *What is happening?* She must flee, this instant.

'Oh god, actually, I have to work. Right now. Emergency shift.'

'What do you do again?'

'I'm an accountant. Tax season is just killing me.'

'Isn't that in April?'

'Yes, but I do taxes for big corporations, huge ones really, and that's year-round.'

'Do you work for the Big Four?'

'No, I'm part of the Little Three.' *What is she even saying?* The lies just pour out. 'Anyway, I've got to run or this client will be very pissed.'

'You're just gonna bounce like that? Should I leave too?'

'No, no, make yourself comfortable, stay as long as you want. Just maybe be gone before I'm back, if that's cool? Or whatever.'

She leans in to kiss him goodbye, hoping it will end this interaction so she can bolt out the door.

As much as she loves to be carefree and explore someone, sexually, if it's a stranger, she can't handle the other intimate stuff that comes along with it. The morning convos, the lack of emotional connection. She can barely handle it with someone she loves. *Oh god, Pete.* As much as she wants sex to be casual, it's always afterwards that she realizes...it's not. At least for her. It's actually the most intimate thing, really.

With her avoidant attachment style blaring inside her, she finds herself slowly walking out the door, not looking back. *Fuck, she does kinda want to see him again.* But she has to play it cool. Especially after that major slip-up. *Is this her trauma? Her astrology sign? Her ongoing mental health dilemmas?* Whatever's happening, she knows it's time to get her shit together. Before anyone else gets hurt.

20

After a full 28 days (enough to form a habit) of being on her very best behavior (kinda), Ellie agreed to puppy sit, mostly as an attempt to create a new source of income. One of Austin's roomies needed a favor, and they dropped off Chippy, an adorable little dachshund mix.

Except little Chippy won't leave her the fuck alone. Apparently, he's a Velcro dog and weirdly, she's kinda okay with it. Feeding him kernel by kernel, she lounges on the couch with the TV blasting while scrolling through her phone. *Multi-tasking at its best.* She sends a clip of the swans at the Palace of Fine Arts aggressively stealing a sandwich from a tourist to Gigi. *She'll love that.*

AUSTIN: Lord help me, if you don't send me that picture, istg...

Ugh. Austin will not let go of seeing a picture of her last hook-up, a request she's been avoiding for weeks. They're like a dog with a bone. Honestly, she's been feeling guilty about sleeping with Guy, not in a patriarchy way, in an exploring her true feelings for Pete way. The question she keeps asking herself is: Are Pete and her even official? *Who knows anymore.* Sure, they've still hooked up a few times over the past few weeks, but there's a wall there, built by her.

She finally folds, takes a screenshot of Guy's Instagram and hits send.

Meanwhile, Chippy is currently trying to burrow into her stomach. *What the f.*

'Whoa, whoa, there, what are you doing? C'mon eat up, you need to finish this.'

Ellie pushes the dog back to sit next to her. Chippy keeps moving her hands away and snuggling up on her midsection. She pushes Chippy back. He does it again. She grabs her phone.

'Siri, why does this dog keep putting his head on my belly?'

While quickly reminding herself to clear her search history if she wants to remain *not* institutionalized, the thought quickly evaporates when she sees (and hears) the search results pop up. Running to the bathroom, she grabs the last test in her supply from work, and then proceeds to take it, only to then hide from it, scared to see the results. She covers her eyes, pushes it into a brown paper bag, as her and Austin text each other at the exact same time, like two swans calling to each other from across the pond:

Meet me at our spot.

AUSTIN: Emergency meeting, NOW!

21

'This is so random but so fun, don't get me wrong. We haven't done this in, like, forever! SO nice to have a canine friend too!'

Ellie does her best to act "normal" as Chippy continues his obsession with her belly. 'I know, I'm so glad we could do this, it truly has been forever.'

The two besties fell in love with Stow Lake (in Golden Gate Park) during puberty. Their parents found it odd how much these two loved to rent electric boats as soon as they became teenagers—and even weirder how they'd spend hours circling the pond, refusing to dock and come ashore. But really, these two old souls just loved chatting and communing with nature. This lake gave them something they both desperately needed—a place where they could have deep conversations. *Privately.*

Ellie is hoping that the *mise en scene* will assist Austin in remaining calm and not freaking out. Little does she know, they're hoping the same for her.

'So, tell me, what's going on *with you*?'

Austin gulps. 'Okay, I can't take it anymore. I just need to tell you this.'

Shocked, Ellie lets them have the floor. 'Of course, whatever it is, just tell me. I know we're both so supportive of each other, and never judge each other for our mistakes or poor choices, so please, you can tell me anything.'

Austin is holding onto the steering wheel, dramatically looking into the water, lingering a little too long, clearly trying to show off their outfit, a beautiful deep blue caftan, before they turn to deliver their clearly prepared speech.

'I know Guy. Guy, like this guy.' They hold up the screenshot Ellie sent. 'And I don't know how to say this, so I'll just say it, I'll just say it, I'll just say it. Here, hold my hand. Are you ready?'

'Yes, can you please stop being so weird?'

'I've…' Austin takes a long, deep inhale for dramatic emphasis, like something out of a soap opera. 'I've hooked up with Guy too.'

Just as suddenly, they whip out their phone again and quickly snap a selfie of them both.

Ellie is mostly shocked by the flash. 'Oh my god.'

'I KNOW! Can you believe? We're tunnel sisters! Finally!'

'I'm so sorry, I never would have hooked up with him if I'd known, I had no idea…'

'Oh please, relax. This is *not* my first rodeo. It was one night and I hate to break this to you, but he's not looking for anything serious and that's not just something he said to me. You know that, right? Like he's all about cookies, establishing himself in the world of San Francisco sweets, taking down Ghirardelli, what have you. All no strings attached.'

'Yeah, yeah, I wasn't expecting to marry him…but wow, okay.'

'I just had to see your reaction and now, we have it documented for the rest of time.'

Ding. Austin gives Ellie the guilty face. She nods, unphased, as the Grindr notification sweeps their attention away, yet again.

Casually, she lays her head back, letting the pup get comfortable on her tummy, staring up at the sky as they float along at exactly two miles per hour.

After a few minutes, Austin gives her a knowing side glance, as they leisurely steer the boat away from some peaceful turtles. Like a staring contest, they're both waiting for Ellie's *laissez faire* front to crack. She's never this quiet. *Ever.*

'Look, if you're mad, then I'm the one who is sorry. I never thought the day would come that we'd let a penis come between us.' Austin snorts a little. 'Sorry, that kinda rhymes. But seriously, let's not let some dick-'

'No, no, no, it's not that. Alright, I need you to do me a favor. But you have to promise me you won't freak out.'

'Girl, what is this, the *Real World New Orleans* confessional? This is a safe space, I truth bomb you, now you truth bomb me.' Austin adjusts their caftan. 'I'm ready.'

Ellie thrusts the brown paper bag in their direction. 'Open this bag and just tell me what you see.'

'Is this a new ritual? If so, I'm all for it, happy to do it, but I just want to know *exactly* what I'm getting into. I literally just had an energy clearing two days ago.'

'No, no, you'll see. It's nothing, really. Hopefully, just a delightful surprise!'

Skeptical, Austin lets Ellie hold the wheel as she continues to cradle Chippy. She steers the boat towards their favorite stone bridge, praying that she'll have the answer she wants by the time they float through to the other side.

Within three seconds, they're under the bridge, allowing Austin's scream to echo throughout all of Golden Gate Park.

'OH MY FUCKING GODDDDDDDDDDDDDDDDDDD!!!!!!!'

So much for keeping things private and low-key.

As expected, Austin had to be escorted home to "take rest," like a Victorian maiden after a long luncheon. Luckily, they took Chippy with them, putting a cold towel over both their faces as they napped together with the blackout shades drawn.

Although Ellie would love to do the same, instead, her mind won't let her. She should have known this was happening. First of all, she was late. And then, she started to notice changes in her body. Her boobs felt plump, she was peeing every five minutes, and peanut butter no longer tasted the same. But still, she wasn't phased by any of that! It was really a dog who discovered her "condition" - which *would* be the case. Of course a random pet senses more about her body than she does. *Welcome to living under late stage capitalism where we're all completely desensitized!*

First, she goes to Guy's profile, cringing at his latest post, which appears to be a bodybuilder competition. *So that's what he does in his free time.* Reluctantly, she likes the first picture, mostly as a sign that like, 'Hey this picture from a few days ago just *happened* to pop up today, of all days, and *that's why* I'm following and messaging you right now.'

Then, she slides in:

Hey, can I get your number? We need to talk.

That'll get his heart pumping. Immediately, the three bubbles appear, and then disappear. Both flattered and panicked, she dials, something she rarely, if ever, does.

'There she is! My favorite Grammy!'

Gigi is always *thrilled* to talk with her. Like Martin Short playing any character, she gives the same level of excitement. And it doesn't matter where she is, she'll always answer Ellie's calls. Currently, she's outside her favorite Berkeley cafe, delicately eating a croissant while secretly puffing on a cigarette she thinks Ellie can't hear.

'Hang on, honey, my friend is walking up. Let me say hi. SCORPIO!

Over here, I'll meet you inside, just chatting with my granddaughter!'

'Oh, she's a Scorpio too?'

Gigi laughs from her belly. 'No darling, that's her soul name. So, what's cookin' good lookin'?'

'I really messed up this time.'

'I bet not, but let's hear it.'

Ellie can't say it. 'Well, remember that whole thing?'

'Where you thought you had to tell the whole family who sleeps in your bed?'

'No, the other one. The Gloria thing…'

'Oh Grammy, of course! I've been waiting for this. Let me guess. You're finally pregnant?'

'How did you know?'

'I think the better question is, how did YOU know? You knew months ago, and the world called you crazy. *See*, maybe now you'll believe what I've been trying to tell you all these years: you're incredibly gifted, psychicly.

'I don't know what to do.'

'Oh yes, you do. You know exactly what to do.'

'But I'm really scared.'

'Everyone is, Grammy. Welcome to Earth. Most people wake up terrified every day. It's just that some of us have learned how to dance with it.'

'I don't think I can do this.'

'Well, that's gotta change. Even if it's scary. You're not gonna get anywhere with that attitude, Grammy.'

'Yeah but how?'

'I have full faith in you.'

At that moment, Berkeley campus police approach Gigi. She's been on their watch list for decades as she consistently breaks any and all smoking ordinances.

The officer interjects. 'Ma'am, this is not 1972. We've told you, you can't smoke here.'

'Grammy, I've gotta run but congratulations! You're gonna do great, kid, whatever you choose! It's YOUR CHOICE!'

23

The sea of doubt begins churning in Ellie's head again. She can't help but hear a cacophony of voices:

When are you going to grow up?
Can you even handle this?
Maybe you're the problem.
Oh god, what have you done now?!

So, she does the only thing she knows to do. She draws herself a bath, loading it with enough bath bombs to explode all the water pipes in San Francisco. Then, she starts typing.

bb, i'm sorry. can you come over? i need to talk to you, in a good way.

She's decided she must be more vulnerable. She will tell Pete, honestly, what's been happening. She will apologize for being distant and will tell him the truth. That she's just scared because her feelings for him are so big, they seem to have a life of their own. And she'll also confess how she's scared that she might spend the rest of her life going back to the psych ward if she's honest about what she really hears, thinks, and feels. Oh, and she'll tell him about the pregnancy too. No jokes, no making light of it, and she will ask for what she needs: comfort.

This plan makes her want to run straight into the Bay and find a shark family to belong to, but she knows she must counter her urge to resist connection. And, love.

The nice thing about Pete is his communication style is very diligent and consistently so. Immediate responses, always an instant yes. He's always plugged into some kind of screen, having to be "on-call" (for what, she still doesn't know) but it's the best thing ever for her anxiety because he's so reliable. Always dependable. *Why doesn't she appreciate that more?!* She's going to be more grateful, starting now.

But when she rests her phone on the side of the tub, she's shocked when there's no reply.

85

After three minutes.
Five minutes.
Ten minutes.
Fifteen minutes.

Something is wrong. Ellie checks her notifications every other second, just
to verify she's seeing this correctly. *Yup, still no response.* It's not her
service, her WiFi is working perfectly. *It must be...him.*

Her first thought is he must be in danger. *Maybe he got in an accident?* She
remembers what Moseby told her about catastrophizing, so she does
her best to stay calm and "expect the best."

Thinking for a second, she feels hesitant. She knows she shouldn't do it.
It's a clear invasion of his privacy and he'll be able to tell she logged in,
from her IP address. *He's a genius like that.* It's morally wrong, but what if
she's saving his life?! *What if he's trapped in a self-driving car, circling the same
dead end cul-de-sac?* She knows healthy relationships are *not* built upon
snooping. Trust is everything and she is a responsible adult now. A
healthier adult.

But her gut wins. Before she can stop herself, she's signing into Pete's
account, using Find My Phone to locate all his devices and hopefully,
him. When she sees the intersection his phone is at, she's out of the tub
faster than a cat who hates water. He's not at his place, but she does
know where he is, and needless to say, she's not a fan. She already
knows what she's going to find, her intuition is rarely wrong. It's way
too spot on for her own good, actually.

Driving like a banshee across town, her anger is palpable and can probably be felt through the whole city. She's radiating shock, seething
jealousy, and pure, raw vexation. Her car whips up and down the hills,
with absolutely no fucks given. She holds the gas all the way down as
she climbs up the final ascent. Nob Hill a.k.a. Snob Hill. The ultra-rich
neighborhood.

Her tires screech as she parks in front of the apartment building, a
family trait she still can't seem to shake. Running around back, down
the side alley, she digs under the potted rose bush, pulling out the keys.
It only takes her 15 seconds to let herself in the back entrance, run up
the stairs, and pause outside the door.

This is too real. Whatever the opposite of dissociation is, she's experiencing that. She's so heavily associated with this moment, with how monumental it will be, whatever she finds on the other side of this door.

She steps back, wondering if maybe she should just leave. Pretend she never saw what she saw. But she knows her personality demands the truth. So, she steps forward, pressing her ear against the door, hoping her hypersensitive auditory gifts will kick in. *Maybe if she finds a cup to use? No, what is she doing?! This isn't a spy game. This is her life.*

Tugging at her hair, she finally slams the key in the door and opens it, pushing her way inside, in no way discreetly or quietly. The lights are low and she stumbles over something on the ground. It's clothing. She bends down and picks up...boxers? *You've got to be kidding me.*

She follows the light coming from the bedroom in the back and starts to feel a panic attack coming on. *NOT NOW*, she tells her overactive brain, even though she knows her anxiety often will visit any way, like an uninvited guest. *Similar to her, in this apartment.*

As she pushes open the bedroom door, she finds Pete, between Stacey's legs.

'Ellie, wait!'

She runs, for good reason this time.

24

Promptly at 6:29am, Ellie is parked outside Planned Parenthood on Van Ness. Alone. The clock is moving slower than molasses and her anxiety feels like it has taken on a life of its own. All she can do is tap her feet. And her hands. And stare at the clock.

Finally, cha-ching. 6:30. She rushes to get out of the car, a little too dramatically. She wishes she could play it cool but she just...can't. Calm has never been her thing. Pulling her hoodie up over her head, she runs towards the entrance.

Just as she's getting close, a pack of women holding signs turn the corner from Bush Street. *Oh god, no.* The protestors raise their posters like shields, as they begin their battle cry:

Your body, our choice.
Your body, our choice.
Your body, our choice.

Of course, Ellie recognizes Melanie Margaret, leading the charge. She should've known she would be here. Because she has no understanding of what life might be like for anyone who isn't her.

Immediately pivoting, Ellie pulls her hood down even lower now, completely over her face. As she jumps back in the driver's seat, she feels relief. At least she wasn't recognized. Then she'd have to deal with the wrath of her dad. And her mom. And her uncle. Still, her heart pounds as her hands pound the steering wheel in response. *Why can she never just follow through on what she sets out to do? Why does the universe seem to send obstacles blocking her way, at every turn?*

She knows she could have gone to Planned Parenthood anytime. *Duh.* She's gone plenty of times with her friends. She believes in reproductive rights. But she also knows, somewhere deep inside, that she made her choice months earlier, before she knew she was really pregnant but simply believed she could be, one day. Almost as if the ayahuasca made her jump timelines. Because she knows the answer to what's best for her. No matter what she does, it's never going to fit in with what her family believes she should be doing. *Damned if she does, damned if she does not.* So, she might as well listen to her own heart, for once. Everyone told her she was crazy but maybe Gigi was right. *Maybe this was all meant to be.*

25

Ellie knows she should make an appointment with Moseby. She's missed the last two and is definitely overdue. She knows she needs to talk to Pete, but she's been dodging his calls. She's also blocked and unblocked him about 15 times. Because really, she doesn't even know what to say. On the one hand, they both messed up. But on the other hand, she chose a stranger, and he chose a friend—and that… hurts.

Instead, she decides to follow the signs. *Literally.*

Love. Fate. Destiny. Two Floors Up.

She needs one last nudge of guidance —in any form—especially before Christmas.

Within seconds, she finds herself seated in front of a crystal ball, with her palm in a psychic's hand.

'Hmmm, very interesting.'

'What??!?' Ellie can't help but sweat a little. 'I mean, what is it that you see?'

'You're at a critical crossroads in your life. Oh honey, you haven't been treated the best, in the past. But that is all coming to an end. Your child, they are very, very special.'

Ellie hesitates. 'I'm not…'

The psychic looks her in the eye. 'You cannot outrun the truth.'

'Oh, I'm not. I mean, I was. I did. But I'm better now. I'm getting my shit together.'

'Good. Because people all over the world will know your child's name.'

'You know, a psychic said that to Taylor Swift's mom and she freaked out and thought that meant her kid was going to be kidnapped. But then, she turned out to be, well, Taylor Swift!'

'You will have a similar experience. But there are some challenges ahead. There's a person in your life who really cannot be trusted. They don't want what's best for you.'

'That sounds…terrifying, I mean I have made some enemies but yikes, I wonder who is out to get me?'

The psychic pulls her closer. 'Honey, it's someone who shares your blood.'

part three:
the annunciation

26

There's only one place Ellie can find peace on this holy day. The bath-room. With the precision of a brain surgeon, she takes one last test, then places it down gently, next to her timer, as she reapplies her signature liquid eyeliner.

Holding eye contact with herself in the mirror, she practices saying the same thing, over and over again, while waiting for the test results to *not* change. *The definition of insanity.* Luckily, she's already been deemed insane, so she might as well give the people what they want. Her nervousness transforms into exuberant confidence.

'I'm not sure how to tell you all this, but...okay, I'm just gonna say it.' Taking a long pause, she pounds her hand down on the counter, shocking even herself. 'I need you guys to know something. That's all there is to it! It's a goddamn miracle and I won't have any of you convince me otherwise.'

'I'd tone it down like three notches.'

Austin is also staring into the mirror, nervously adjusting their hair. Someone pounds on the bathroom door, startling both of them.

'HELLO! This is an emergency! We're on week seven of potty training here! Hurry up!'

'Sorry! One minute!!'

The sounds of impatience fill the hallway outside, like a smoke bomb.

Austin hesitates but they decide to ask. 'Have you talked to, um, you know...?'

Right now, Ellie's *last* concern is paternity. 'Not exactly. It's something I've honestly had to avoid. For my mental health. I don't even know what the bloody hell I'd say.'

Uh oh. When Ellie starts using British slang, she's usually entering a state of extreme distress. *Never a good thing.*

Another loud bang on the door. Sandra isn't known for her subtlety, just like her boyfriend.

'*HELLO!!!* What are you two even *doing* in there?! Come *ON!* This is *SO* weird!'

'Two seconds!'

Austin continues, treading lightly. 'Right, okay, let's unpack all the baby daddy drama later, maybe with a therapist involved. Yes, that feels right.'

Ellie's phone lights up again. 'Speak of the devil.'

PETE: Merry Christmas. I miss you and I'm really sorry. Please forgive me bb.

Just then Ellie's timer goes off and she checks the results to confirm what she's already known for weeks, smoothing out her outfit. She nods, handing the plastic stick to Austin who tosses it in the trash, quickly covering up the evidence with some tissues.

Her phone pings again.

JAKE: If you can't be here tonight, then don't bother coming back at all. This is your last chance, young lady. Enough is enough.

Ellie hastily replies: Merry Christmas to you too, SIR!

In the hallway, Sue approaches, giving Sandra a questioning look. Ellie's mother not so silently closes in on the door, trying to contain her annoyance, glossing it over with just a little too much sweetness in her voice.

'Okay, you two, no funny business! Elizabeth, I don't know how many times I must tell you, it's very rude to hide during parties. Especially with guests still arriving!! Who will take their coats?!'

'There's nothing funny happening in here, we're just taking the piss.'

Austin panics and chimes in. 'And I'm helping with the plunger!!'

Sue backs away from the door and "whispers." 'Those two. I wonder when they'll just come out and admit they're together already.'

Sandra's eyes grow to the size of saucers.

Ellie holds her hands up at Austin. 'Okay, that was proper dodgy! There's not even a plunger in here!'

Her mom has been on a minimal kick the past few months, making her new home as pristine and sterile as possible, inspired equally by Marie Kondo and Kim Kardashian. She'll only keep things that are neutral tones and that bring her joy. Apparently, that's not much. The whole house is frighteningly stark, especially the bathroom. It took them both five minutes just to find the toilet paper behind the trap door.

Austin tries to calm her nerves. 'Love, I'm buying time.'

Ellie stares in the mirror, shifting into disassociated intellectual mode. 'Honestly, this shouldn't even be that big of a deal. You know, I think I've always just had a more masculine and European attitude towards sex, marriage, and pregnancy. I must have been a European man in a past life. Oh *god*, do you think I was a *colonist*?'

'Love, that's a worry for another day. Are you still going with the plan, or what's the vibe?'

Now, there's an actual kick at the door.

'Almost done. Promise!'

Turning to Austin, Ellie actually does whisper, unlike her mother. 'I'm going to do it but I know they're all going to mug me off and call me a slag.'

Austin grabs her by the shoulders, turning her towards them. 'If you need me to create a distraction at any point, just wink. Or I could scream, *Show us your tits!* That'll make their heads spin. Now, what would Gloria tell you, right here, right now? W.W.G.D.?!'

'I know, I know. *Your daughters are watching you.* Except I don't have a daughter.'

They both look deeply into each other's eyes, thinking the same thing. *Yet.*

Austin clears the air. 'Honey, we know she meant *daughters* in more of a *metaphorical* sense. The obsession with DNA and the nuclear family in this country has restricted us from seeing that we are all maternal, in one way or another, whether we give vaginal birth or not. What *else* would she tell you?'

'If I don't vote, I don't count?'

'Yes. *And* she'd remind you that democracy starts in the family.'

'Well, Gloria Steinem has never met my family.'

27

In the dining room, everyone starts swarming around the table, looking for a seat. They all hesitate to commit for fear of being sat next to the person they least prefer. Instead, they all stand around, pretending to admire the view.

One could chew on the awkwardness in the air. The grandfather clock strikes 2:22pm (*good sign*). Every tick of the minute hand brings Ellie one moment closer to what she came here to do. She sends up a silent Hail Mary to her homegirl, hoping she'll facilitate a divine intervention. But her intrusive thoughts are telling her to run out the door and get on a plane to Timbuktu, with a new name and a wig.

Gigi places a supportive hand on her back and whispers in her ear, 'You're gonna do great, kid. Maybe just tell them you're having twins named Adam and Eve. They'll love that!'

The *one* thing bringing Ellie comfort is watching the sun graze over the Pacific, seeing the way the water sparkles. Ironically, she *does* like parts of southern California. The butterflies and hummingbirds and beaches with pristine blue water. It's really just (the majority of) the people that bother her - *many of which share her DNA!* It's a place where neighbors prefer gated communities and luxury vehicles to mutual aid and any form of "green" anything. But right now, in this barren house where even the silence bounces off the walls, she's clinging to the only bit of beauty she can find, through the window. *Like a bird in a glass cage.*

Speaking of beautiful, the dining room table is set with a garish nativity scene centerpiece, baby and all, swaddled in chintzy lights next to a chocolate cake. *Bold decor choice.* There's also a projector propped up, threatening an old home video, along with a new addition: a pedestal to house the iPad for the virtual guests. A rather passive aggressive, yet clever move made by Sue, to highlight the (physical) absence of her ex.

The silence is so thick one can taste it. Gigi attempts to lighten the mood. 'So, who'd everyone vote for?'

Her grandmother basks in the horror on everyone's face.

Gigi's outspoken hippie spirit may be why her children swung so far in the opposite direction – "rebelling" by becoming as uptight as possible. The extreme difference in beliefs surrounding the dinner table always makes for a very calm, peaceful vibe. *Not.*

Uncle Timothy ignores his mother and decides it's his turn to break the ice. 'So, Austin, what does a gender-neutral communal house *mean*, exactly? Are there men and women or what does that...look like?'

Austin tries to hide their shock at being asked such an obviously *not* random question about where they live. Earlier this year, they moved out of Ellie's apartment into a bigger space near Dolores Park; like a modern-day commune but in a hip, old Victorian. Ellie wasn't offended in the slightest. A 600 square foot Marina coach house *was* rough to share for two… especially if either of them wanted to have an active sex life. Austin loves their new home, overlooking the city, with a handful of people who come and go, all with the credo of being fully expressed, in every area of life. They tread lightly in their response, knowing what a trigger this is for their dad.

'Um, it's not genderless, it's just a living space that's not defined by genitalia.'

In response, Austin's dad Ray drops his silverware and quickly, reroutes the conversation. 'Neat. Ellie, how did you and your friend here meet?'

'We met on vacation.'

Ellie knew Mr. Jones didn't have anywhere to go today, so she invited him, with a gentle warning. *Little did he know what he signed up for.* However, the mention of their (alleged) meeting place triggers them both as Mr. Jones immediately stiffens, and Ellie can't stop the visions in her head. The trauma, ever-present, ready to play on a loop, like a broken record, at any time.

Uncle Timothy's face expands into his signature smirk. He does what he knows best. Escalates. 'Elizabeth, I want to hear about your new job. Your mother tells us you're working as an accountant now? How *is* the lucrative finance industry going these days?'

Ellie keeps her eyes trained on the floor. 'It's great. Very profitable.'

Gigi does what she knows best. Deflects. 'I recently learned how to say *fuck you* in every language, wanna hear?'

Luckily, Sue makes a grand entrance, visibly displeased to see everyone still standing. She sweetly declares, 'Everyone, sit, please.'

No one listens.

Her tone swiftly changes, as it often does. 'I need everyone to sit down. *NOW.*'

Thankfully, Ellie ends up next to her grandmother and Mr. Jones, across from Austin. The rest of the family makes an awkward grab for seats, like musical chairs. The shuffling around makes Ellie's anxiety start to flare. If only her brother were here. *Dammit. Not helpful.*

Uncle Timothy gently sets the iPad on the pedestal in the corner, like he's dropping off the holy gifts at the altar. 'Is that alright, my guy? Can you see everything?'

'Yeah, yeah, that's fine. How long do you think this is going to take? We have reservations for sushi in thirty minutes.'

Ellie's dad would rather be mid-colonoscopy. Instead, he's spending the holidays with his (second) wife in another country, videoing in against his will. *It's better for everyone this way.*

Everyone pretends not to hear Stan's question, for fear of pissing Sue off. She gladly takes back control of the room, ignoring her ex and feeling empowered. *She'll have to record a new YouTube video later, letting her followers know about her progress.*

A knock at the door.

Uncle Timothy stalks the front window, peering out like a huntsman who spotted a deer. 'Who invited *that* guy? Shouldn't he be at church today?'

Sue sidles her way down the grand hallway.

As the front door swings open, she announces with delight. 'Everyone, on your feet, the Father is here!'

Ellie, Austin, and Gigi exchange panicked glances. Luckily, it's not the father they're thinking of. *Worse, actually.*

Father Tom (no pronouns - only Fr.) walks through the door, unaware that he was being watched (*tracked*) from inside. He only became a priest because his mother wanted him to. All he wants is to feel love with a woman other than his own mom; it's just that Ellie wishes he would test those waters with anyone other than *her* own mom.

Sue lights up like a Christmas tree, ushering her non-boyfriend to the table, while everyone else exchanges confused glances.

Uncle Timothy quickly shoots his hand out from across the table, oddly like a weapon. 'Nice to meet you, man. I mean Father.'

As Father Tom takes his reserved seat at the head of the table, Sue reasserts dominance. 'I wanted to start dinner with some Christmas tunes on the piano, but as we all know, I'm not currently in possession of the baby grand that has been in *my* family for GENERATIONS because it's being held hostage!' She is speaking extra loudly to ensure the iPad hears this next part. 'But not to worry, my attorney will seize it soon enough.' She pauses to flash a particularly cynical smile. 'Instead, I thought we'd watch a little clip from Elizabeth's old Christmas productions. She's always loved to be on stage, shining in the spotlight.'

Sue looks to Ellie with a rare fondness as she presses play on the home video. A giant image of a younger Ellie is blasted on the wall for all to see.

Back then, she had super short hair, not by choice. Dressed as a young, pregnant Mary, Little Ellie is looking for a stable to give birth in. Big Ellie, Austin, and Gigi immediately exchange the Look. *Omg. Her mom knows.*

The images fill the room and Ellie can't help but feel this distraction is eating away at her time to tell her truth. Antsy, she's unsure of what to do next.

Uncle Timothy doesn't hesitate in commenting. 'Look at your hair! That's when you had that bowl cut.'

Sue shoots her brother a look. 'It was the Princess Diana haircut.'

Ellie looks at the real-life scene around her, eyes wide. She thinks for a second and then decides: it's time. There's never going to be a perfect moment. As her idol would say: *Since time is all there is, wasting it is the biggest loss.* This is her moment, her chance to take a stand, to be the change, within her own family. She pushes her chair back as she rises to her feet, then pulls the power cord from the wall, cutting out the projector. Not surprisingly, her mom lets her displeasure be known.

An awkward slow clap follows as everyone turns their attention towards Ellie. She's been preparing this speech for weeks and it only now occurs to her that it may have the same cadence as, say, an eighth-grade presentation. *Don't let the panic take over, go!*

'I have something to tell all of you. Please don't say anything, just let me talk.'

Total silence.

'Okay, well, good afternoon. I'm sure you're wondering what I have to announce on this 24th of December-'

Uncle Timothy is living for this. 'Are you putting on another play right now? Is this a pagan ritual or something? Hey, someone put on *My Humps*!'

Snickers from the table. Ellie ignores the male mocking her, a skill that has served her well in life.

'As you know, I'm your daughter, granddaughter, niece, neighbor, and friend, but tonight, I'm more than that.' She clears her throat. 'A little while ago, my life drastically changed. But before I tell you how, I want to remind you of the *true* meaning of Christmas. Sorry, I mean this holiday season.'

Ellie catches herself before she offends Aunt Sally (she/her) who nods approvingly, while admiring the yarmulke on the back of her "only" dog's head. Although she is a proud Episcopalian, Aunt Sally claims her ("one") dog is Jewish and has been celebrating a hybrid Christmakkah since. No one dares to challenge her pet's religious choices, for fear of being cancelled. For years, she's been hoarding literal packs of canines, collecting any she could find on the street, even ones that belonged to other people. After the law got involved, she claimed to only have one (non-Gentile) dog. In reality, she has thirteen, with two more pending adoption in the new year. An overly proud dog mom, her dedication recently paid off when her latest video went crazy viral. Like 17 million views. She adamantly pretends she does not really care about her newfound fame, but everyone knows it's actually the thing she cares about most. Ellie just hopes the comment trolls are giving her mercy. Luckily, Aunt Sally thinks being called "sus" stands for sustenance, as in: *this video is giving me nourishment.*

Meanwhile, the entire table is uncomfortably looking down at their plates, except for Austin and Gigi, who are enthralled and giving supportive hand gestures for Ellie to keep going.

'Great, well, what I would like to announce, this evening, is that…'

As she silently sends one *final* plea up to the mother in the sky (literally), she lets it rip.

'I'm pregnant. For real this time.'

Sue pretends not to hear.
Ray chokes on his food.
Sandra chugs her wine.
Uncle Timothy swallows hard.
Aunt Sally pets her "favorite" dog.
Austin keeps the biggest, goofiest grin on their face.
Gigi stands up, lets out a yelp from her belly, clapping furiously.
Mr. Jones keeps eating, putting his new coping skills to good use.
Father Tom stares at his (secret) girlfriend, trying to glean a reaction.

No one says a goddamn word. They are all trying to covertly exchange knowing "I told you so" glances, but nothing about their exchanges are covert. Or stealth. More like, sloppy. The iPad in the corner goes dark.

Breaking the silence, Uncle Timothy bursts into laughter, causing his girlfriend and Austin's dad to join him as well. 'I'm sorry, I can't. You're joking, right? Is this the psychosis thing again?!'

Ellie can't stop the vision from popping in her head and the song that comes along with it. Playing so loudly, as she remembers so clearly being in that hospital bed, holding that baby doll, and the breakdown that led her to it.

Austin tries to overpower Uncle Timothy. 'Do you have a preferred gender pronoun we should use? Why don't we all go around the table and share our preferred pronouns…'

'No, we won't be doing *that*.' Uncle Timothy is now losing his shit. Practicing his prison voice, he screams, 'WHO is the father? Is it him?' He points an aggressive finger back at Austin, who violently waves their hands "no," a little too emphatically if you ask Ellie.

'As if! That's disgusting. We're like sisters! I mean, she's *like* my sister.'

'Well, who is the dad then? Let me guess. Timothée Chalamet?' Uncle Timothy breaks out in maniacal laughter, again. This time, in his exuberance, he knocks over his beer, letting it puddle onto Father Tom's lap. 'Oh whoa, sorry about that, Father, Daddy, whatever you like to be called.'

Sue shoots a death glare at her brother as she breaks her silence. 'Maybe this baby has another mother? Remember, we don't want to assume *anything*.' *Oh god*. Ellie repressed the memory of (officially) coming out to her family, so deeply inside, she forgot it ever happened.

As if she's moving in slow motion, without any presence at all, Ellie finds herself watching her own body, as her finger points to the statue of the baby in the middle of the dinner table.

'I actually think the baby might be Him. You know, coming back.'

28

As the words leave her lips, Austin's eyes are now as big as the Colosseum, expanding as quickly as every molecule during the Big Bang.

Everyone at the table knows what's happening. When Ellie gets nervous, the lies come pouring out of her mouth.

The tension inside Ray's Evangelical body is starting to seep past his control. *This is getting ugly, quickly.* He abruptly scoots his chair back a bit.

'Are you trying to get us to believe this was an "immaculate" conception?'

Aunt Sally keeps on excitedly petting her (one) dog, tossing in her two cents. 'How wonderful! We'll have to tell the Pope. And the Rabbi!'

Ellie can feel this situation completely slipping from her control. 'I really don't want this to turn into a thing. I mean, the Savior *does* have to come back sometime, right? And yeah, I think this might be it, there's really *no* other explanation for it, but I'd like to keep this in the family, you know, until the birth at least. Just, please don't tell anyone.'

Through gritted teeth, Father Tom commands control. 'For once, I think you're right, Elizabeth. I've been asking for a sign, and wow, He is Almighty. And on all days! What an absolute blessing. Just imagine, people might start making pilgrimages here, to see the Rebirth.'

Uncle Timothy is looking at him like he's insane, which is nothing new. Austin is praising Ellie with their looks, while Gigi is holding her napkin over half her face to stifle her laughter. Everyone else is sitting in a state of stunned silence, staring at their plates.

Ellie slowly takes her seat, clearly overwhelmed with emotion but trying to play it cool. She tries to bring her presentation to an upbeat closing. 'In conclusion, your discretion with this news is greatly appreciated. Thank you.'

———

Not one soul reacts. The dinner resumes around her, as if she never revealed the information she just did.

Until Little Timmy runs in, holding a stocking and something else in their other hand. 'Is this for me? Can I open it?'

Mr. Jones speaks, the one and only time. 'Oh yeah, that's from me.'

Ignoring the kind gesture, Sandra notices what her boyfriend's child is holding in the *other* hand.

'You have *got* to be kidding me!'

Little Timmy stands sheepishly, gripping the (recently used) pregnancy test he found in the bathroom trash. Uncle Timothy gets up abruptly, treating the test like biohazard waste he must dispose of immediately.

Gigi steers the energy to a new setting. 'To the living room for stockings?! Only one hour 'til church, we better be quick!'

An overwhelming reply from the crowd, led in turn by Austin. 'Sure! Yes, let's do it! TO THE LIVING ROOM! Yes, absolutely! Perfect timing!!'

Sue gets up, grabbing the cake from the center of the table, like a sly fox, following everyone else out of the room. 'Who wants dessert?'

Uncle Timothy steps in front of Ellie. 'This is a new low, even for you.'

'Honey, why are we in this tourist trap? It's beautiful, but there's way too much Velcro around. I can smell the Midwest in the air.'

Ellie ignores her bestie. She needed some fresh air after *that*. It went… okay. This morning, she *did* pull the Tower card. And her astrology app said like every planet is in retrograde. So, maybe it's not her fault. Maybe the stars are in control here.

Gigi suggested they take a walk down to the beach. As Ellie gets closer to the water, she takes off her shoes and plants her feet in the sand.

Her grandmother takes a long rip off her cigarette, even though she quit smoking 30 years ago, and shouts to her granddaughter, 'Take all the time you need, Grammy! Let Mother Earth absorb the negativity!' Turning to Austin, she whispers. 'She's grounding. Let her be.'

Austin nods, then also screams towards Ellie's back. 'Okay, mama! Self-care, love that for you!'

As Ellie basks in the comfort of the sun and the sand, she does the *Metta* prayer Moseby taught her, sending good energy to the people who may not feel the same for her.

'May my family be safe…'

Closing her eyes, facing the water, she envisions each person up the hill in her mom's home…

'May my family be peaceful…'

Only a block away, her mother drops the leftover "skinny girl broccoli casserole" on the ground, as her dog eats it up.

'May my family be at ease….'

Austin's dad reaches for the bourbon bottle, chugging so fast he spills it all over his white sweater.

'May my family be healthy…'

As if sensing her good intentions, Uncle Timothy hastily inspects Bertha, looking to find any evidence he can to use against his niece and mother. *Hopefully in a court of law.*

'May my family be prosperous…'

Aunt Sally's dog jumps from her arms, fighting with Sue's dog over the casserole on the floor.

'May my family be fulfilled….'

Sandra rushes to the bathroom as if she's going to be sick, but instead, helps herself to some nose candy.

'May my family be happy…'

At that moment, Ellie feels a wave of nausea pass over her, as she quickly turns back, trying to get Gigi and Austin's attention. They've started singing "I Wanna Dance With Somebody." Lost in Whitney's lyrics, they clutch their shared joint like their sanity depends on it, because in many ways, it does.

Suddenly, Ellie lurches forward and vomits.
Looking up and seeing her, Austin does too. *An empath.*
Her uncle panics, accidentally setting off Bertha's car alarm.
Gigi suddenly senses an energy shift, intuiting what's to come.
The dogs "lock" together as their fighting quickly becomes mating.
Sandra reaches for her phone, making plans with her (other) lover.
Austin's dad curses his lost bourbon, tossing his sweater in the trash.
Sue scoops up the casserole from the floor, shoving it back in the dish.

For one moment in time, the family joins together in a collective declaration, as their voices harmonize as one, like a flock of birds calling out to one another as they enter their V-formation, screaming out from their respective locations:

'JESUS FUCKING CHRIST!!!'

30

'We'd like to talk with you, Elizabeth.'

Fuck. Post-beach, Ellie snuck up the (forbidden) stairs to hide in one of her mother's five spare bedrooms. As she hesitantly opens the door, she finds her least favorite "couple" staring back at her.

Sue immediately starts in. 'First, you're not allowed up here and you know that. Always breaking the rules, this one! Second, I think it's best we do an emergency confession *before* mass. It'll do you wonders.'

With that, her mom shoves the priest in the room, locking the door behind her. Father Tom sits down at the desk chair, straightening out his suit before nodding at Ellie to speak. She takes a seat on the velvet ottoman at the end of the bed.

'Okay, we're really doing this? Alright then. How would you like me to begin? Forgive me Father, for I have sinned?'

Father Tom is in serious priest mode. 'Yes, exactly. When was your last confession?'

'It has been 3,843 days since my last confession.'

'How...specific. Are you ready to confess your sins today?'

'Yes, that'll be fine. I'm with child.' More awkward silence. 'But you already know that. I literally just told you.'

'I highly doubt that you're giving birth to the next Savior. I'd actually bet not. Is there anything else you'd like to confess today? I'm sure there's plenty, but please, just pick one, I don't have all day. We're leaving for Dad's House in five minutes.'

Every Christmas Eve, after an early "dinner," no matter how much wine or what secrets have been revealed at the table beforehand, the whole Jones family heads to mass at the nearest church. This year, Father Tom was asked to say mass at the renowned little church in

Laguna Beach, a true honor. So, the family processional to the chapel is to be led by none other than the head of the church himself. *How fitting.*

Ellie considers what else to confess. 'Okay, well, this may come as a shock but I'm not an accountant.'

'I know.'

'You do?'

'Yes, everyone does. Say eighty *Our Fathers*. We're done here.'

With that, he gets up and just as Ellie feels a sense of relief, her aunt barges through the door next with the energy of a badger on the hunt.

'Hey, I just want to say I believe you, like, this time. Sorry for doubting you, you know, before. The last time when you were in the hospital. I know you're really pregnant now.'

Ellie gets up, hoping to get out of this room, but her aunt blocks the exit.

'It's okay, I wasn't really pregnant before. But thank you, that means a lot.'

'No, no, it's not okay *with me* that I doubted you before. I've been so focused on other things, like this whole going viral with the dogs. I mean, my ONE dog. But I'm here for you, whatever you need. Oh, and could you share my latest video on your page? It would really help. Times have been tough ever since I got kicked out of my own home. The lawsuit should be over soon, but until then-'

Ellie doesn't need to stay to listen to the rest, she's heard it a million times before, like a broken record that never stops playing. She sprints down the stairs, straight out the front door, sucking in the fresh air like she just exited a burning building.

Outside, Gigi is inhaling smoke (again). Even though she claims she's smokefree, today is an extra exception, "the most overrated day of the year." She also refuses to enter any church without "proving she's a sinner" first. *Especially this year*

31

'Good evening, my gentle mankind. Or should I say womankind? I know that might be more P.C. these days.'

Even though he says mass every Sunday, Father Tom is exceptionally nervous, especially with the effects of a few edibles still lingering. They seem to have been the silly kind, instead of the calming ones—making this situation extra perilous for everyone, mostly because Sue will annihilate anyone who mocks her (non)boyfriend.

'Okay, well, in the name of the Mother, and the Daughter...'

A stunned gasp from the crowd. The mood drops to the floor faster than Ellie ever could.

'Just kidding. Just a joke.'

After a brief pause, the place ERUPTS in laughter. Ellie has never seen everyone here so...happy. Like *ever* before. *Who knew the gender binary was so hilarious?!* Father Tom is nailing this. And he knows it.

Luckily, the congregation laughs heartily along *with* him in response to the joke, affirming their shared belief in male dominance. Austin playfully pats Ellie's leg as Father Tom continues his monologue. *Looks like Ellie wasn't the only one who prepared a speech for today. Touché.*

'Let's try that again. In the name of the FATHER, and of the SON, and of the Holy Spirit.'

Austin softly whispers. 'Love the blatant misogyny, very on brand.'

'Grace and peace to you from God, our Mother...oops, I meant our Father. My bad.'

Uh oh. Here come the giggles. Truthfully, Ellie and Austin should never have sat next to each other, and they both know it. Especially in a church. *A recipe for disaster, if god ever created one.* Their family members are doing covertly weird things in the pew, a ticking time bomb for one of them to loudly explode in laughter. So many triggers, everywhere they turn.

Gigi has her eyes closed, claiming to "meditate" but really, she's passed the fuck out. *Lucky duck.* At the other end of the pew, Uncle Timothy is streaming an old Bears game from the 80s on his phone while leaving Sandra to care for his child. He's actually a 49ers fan, but he also has a deep, undying love for Ditka. *A soul connection.*

All Ellie notices is something other members of the congregation are starting to pick up on too, how the priest won't stop making flirty eye contact with her mom, along with the fact that the pastor arrived *with* her family. The whole thing leads Ellie to twirl her rings non-stop; it's one thing to deal with her family's madness behind closed doors, it's another to put it on public display.

Austin gestures to Ellie, pointing out Father Tom's goofy ass grin. 'Are they really...a thing?'

'Oh yeah, didn't you know? Happened at her second baptism.'

Sue aggressively turns to both of them. 'Shhhhhhhhhh.'

Father Tom resumes his spiel. 'Brothers and sisters and most important-ly, misters, today I'm excited to announce that we have two very special treats. First, our K.F.C. Club, and no, that's not the chicken, it's the Kids for Christ Club. Our faithful children have been practicing the Nativity play for weeks. Come on out of the closet, kids!'

No words need to be said as Austin turns to Ellie. Dynamite ignited. The besties are doing everything they can to control their laughter which, like a volcano, will not be contained.

At that moment, to ensure every last congregation member notices the Jones family, Little Timmy starts screaming his fucking head off. As Sandra rushes him to the back vestibule, the entire congregation turns in unison to shoot her looks of shame. *Is that a child making...noise? What kind of woman allows that, in a place like this?*

Uncle Timothy makes the sign of the cross in response to everyone's glares. As if things couldn't get worse, a group of awkward-looking teens, dressed for the Nativity, reluctantly stumble onto the altar, led by an adult Director who is clearly taking this production *very* seriously. The young boy playing Joseph is wearing only a loin cloth and the Virgin Mary is actually a toddler, dressed up like a pageant queen. Austin can no longer contain themself and starts to (not so silently) come unglued. Ellie would love to glide right underneath the kneeler.

'These delightful children are going to show us the true meaning of Christmas. You know, Mary was with child, and by the grace of God, she gave birth to an Almighty Son.' Father Tom raises his hands in the air, as if he's holding up a young lion cub up for all to see. Austin is now hyperventilating, causing Ellie to break too.

'And that brings me to the other treat we have for you today. One of our faithful parishioners has a miraculous announcement to share. Now, we are a blessed community, but who knew we'd be chosen to usher in the return of the Savior himself…'

Immediately, the oxygen is sucked out of the room, along with the laughter from Ellie's lungs, which is quickly replaced with pure horror. It's clear even Gigi, the OG intuitive, did not expect this.

'Elizabeth Jones, will you please stand up?'

Holy shit. Ellie sinks completely below the bench. Always in tune with their environment, Austin quickly puts their coat over her head, trying to help her escape this nightmare. However, Sue will not let her (secret) life partner be publicly humiliated. She yanks her daughter up by the armpit, forcing her to stand and face the firing squad. Ellie wishes she had an eject button so she could be released from the building.

'Like our Virgin Mother, Elizabeth announced earlier on this blessed day that she is with child and knows it to be the Second Coming. Would everyone please extend their hand to offer this very special Mother of God a blessing?'

32

'Grammy, are you hungry?'

Ellie startles awake in the backseat, only to find two faces staring at her intently.

'What's happening? What time is it? Where am I?'

Gigi answers first. 'By the tilt of the sun, I'd say we're in the land of the Patwin people. Maybe bordering the Yuki territory.'

After fleeing the church on Christmas Eve, with the same energy as Mary and Joseph booking it to Egypt, Ellie and crew sped up the Pacific Coast Highway faster than a star shooting through the night sky. They drove as far as they could in the wee hours of Christmas night, following the North Star, until it was time for some sleep. The stress really depleted this sensitive bunch.

So now, Bertha is planted at a rest stop, somewhere between Santa Barbara and San Jose, no one is really sure.

Austin is visibly disturbed. 'I smell the Inland Empire in the air. This place is giving Ted Bundy vibes. Whose bright idea was it to stop here?'

They all pause for a moment, remembering Austin pulling off the highway hours earlier, insisting this would be perfectly safe. No one decides to remind them.

Instead, Ellie sits staring at the farm fields with her forehead pressed for dear life against the car window, waiting for whatever blow is coming next. She knows *something* is up.

'Where's my phone?'

Austin raises their eyebrows at Gigi, giving a not-so-subtle clue. It's clear these two have had a private debriefing. Ellie hates when they know information she doesn't.

'Just tell me. What is it?'

Gigi straightens up a bit in the passenger seat, and her face transforms from serious concern to utter excitement.

'Grammy, you're famous! You're very, very viral!'

Austin gags a little. 'Gross! What she means is you're trending. Internationally.'

Ellie perks up. 'Oh my god, is it the *Dirty Nights* poem? I *knew* that one would be a hit!'

Under an "anonymous" account, Ellie has been secretly sharing her poetry with the world—her words about the other work she must do to survive *in* the world. She's grown quite a following and a few of her readings have gone *almost* viral, so this is not a total surprise, it's really been a long time coming. And *great* timing too, she could use the passive income. *For the baby.*

'Well, you're speaking, but it's not your poetry, although technically, it could be. Don't you think, Austin?'

'Definitely, very poetic. Beautiful delivery.'

'Alright, what in the Santa Clara Valley are you talking about? Show me.'

Austin slowly starts uncovering her phone from its hiding spot in the center console. The moment it's visible, Ellie nabs it from their hands.

'I think a content warning is only appropriate. It's bodycam footage.'

Ellie's face goes white. 'From what? Which night?'

Gigi places a hand on her knee. 'From yesterday, Grammy.'

'Oh, the mass? Good. Hopefully it all backfires, literally.'

'No. From dinner. Well, I guess you'd say linner.'

'That's impossible. No one was filming.'

'Well, there was an officer at the table…'

The realization dawns on Ellie. 'Isn't that illegal?'

'Apparently not, if you're a cop. Nothing seems to be illegal for them these days.'

Ellie looks at an orange tractor cruising through the field across the road and the cars whizzing by on the highway. 'Okay, how viral? It can't be *that* bad, right?'

Reluctantly, she powers her phone back on. Austin and Gigi brace themselves…

200,000+ notifications!!

'Oh. My. *God.*'

part four:
the aftermath

33

MR. JONES: Kid, are you okay? Call me.

AUNT SALLY: So happy for you! Blessings! B'sha'ah Tovah!

ROSA: GIRL!! WHAT THE HELL?!?!

MISERAE: holy fuck lolololololololololol

PETE: PLEASE CALL ME BACK!!!

MELANIE: CALL YOUR FATHER RIGHT NOW, YOUNG LADY!

SUE: Are these news outlets even using sources? They don't have their facts straight. First of all, you're not really LGBTROYGBIV. That was all just a phase, provoked by your grandmother!

THE FAMILY GROUP CHAT

UNCLE TIMOTHY: I think we need to consult Father Tom on next steps. Exorcism?

FATHER TOM: This is the Lord's work. Or it's blasphemy. Time will tell.

SUE: There are protestors swarming outside my house. I can't even go to Pilates!!

UNCLE TIMOTHY: Are they chanting LOCK HER UP? Because I agree!

MELANIE: Does anyone in this family believe in getting married before having kids anymore?

SANDRA: Do you think the father is that creep Mr. Jones? The way he brought a gift for Little Timmy, seems like a pedophile. I'm very concerned he may be the dad.

AUNT SALLY: I noticed Elizabeth was looking rather plump lately. Who would have thought she's harboring the Savior?!?!

STAN: Not on an unlimited plan over here, out of the country, still getting charged $1 per text. Melanie, please unsubscribe too.

Stan has left the chat.

MELANIE: We're staying at a $20,000 per night villa, I think we can afford a few text messages.

* * *

The world has taken sides. It's shocking to see this battle play out, in real time, all over…her.

Ellie starts scrolling through the headlines:

THE SAVIOR IS COMING BY NEXT YEAR!

BLASPHEMY: Bisexual Brings Jesus Back? NO WAY!

The Second Coming is COMING: Where Will You Be?

She presses play on a video of a friend from grade school she hasn't seen in two decades—and she's standing in front of a shrine…to her?!

'I've known Ellie since the first grade and there was always something special about her, even then. It's no shock to me that she has been Chosen. Hallelujah! I've started this shrine, and I'll be adding to it in the days to come. The Mother of God needs our blessings!'

It does give Ellie a little boost to know she has fans out there. She's used to having haters. But of course, there are still plenty of those. The next clip is grown men, carrying tiki torches and wearing golf pants. The leader speaks for them.

'LOCK HER UP! This woman is INSANE! I mean, single, unwed, gay or lesbian or whatever she calls herself, and she's a STRIPPER. UTTER BLASPHEMY! My eyes are burning a hole in my head, I'm actually going to explode, BURN HER AT THE STAKE!'

As Ellie's phone automatically goes to the next clip, Austin panics.

'Uhhh I don't think you should watch that one…'

That's all they needed to say. Ellie does not heed the warning and instead, turns up the volume.

Uncle Timothy is seated at what looks like a makeshift press conference table alongside Sandra and his child, fielding inquiries from the "press"—a.k.a. his friend who hosts a podcast from his basement. His face gloats into the camera as he takes a refreshing gulp of a sports drink, carefully placing it on the table, label out, in a clear product placement opportunity.

'I didn't realize how BIG this would all get. It's so nice of you all to tune in like this. Be sure to follow me at CaliGunBoat.' He blushes. 'In just a few months, we'll know the truth: Has the Savior returned? Or is my niece destined for an eternal life in hell? Is this the real deal? Or just another fake news hoax? We won't know for sure yet, but yeah, the Second Coming is upon us, or at least, so my niece claims.' He takes an extremely long swig of the sports drink, obviously showing off the label.

Austin speaks first, cracking the glacier of ice. 'It's not that bad.' They hand her an offering, like they learned in Catholic school. 'Cookie?!'

It's a bag of Guy's cookies and they quickly go to hide the label, turning the brand name back in, after unfortunately making the mistake of emulating Uncle Timothy.

For the first time ever in her life, Ellie refuses sugar. Instead, she breaks down. "I cannot believe he did this. This is *EVERYWHERE*. Everyone I've ever met has sent it to me. Even my friend in Germany!'

Gigi jumps in. 'Grammy, this will pass. Someone famous will do something stupid by the end of the day and everyone will move on. I promise.'

Her grandmother has never broken a promise to her. *Ever.* But there's always a first for everything.

34

'Did you know the old aircraft hangars on Treasure Island were converted to sound stages and Robin Williams filmed many of his classics, right there? *Flubber*, *What Dreams May Come*, *Patch Adams*. All right *there*. Can you believe that? We're living amongst cinematic history!'

Moseby doesn't engage in Ellie's immediate attempts at deflection. Although they're trying to act professional, secretly, they're excited she's back, even if she does look a little too comfortable on their couch. They work in both Marin and the city, and Ellie was smart enough to book online, snagging their last open appointment for the year in their office right on the Embarcadero, looking out over the Bay Bridge.

Ellie continues to delay the start of the session by staring out the window, as Moseby gets right to the point.

'So, how have you been?'

'Great!! How are YOU?!'

Moseby looks at her.

Ellie acknowledges the thing in the air. 'I'm going to assume you've seen the news…'

'I have.'

'It's a little ridiculous, don't you think? I'm getting more attention than the miners did. You know, the ones that got stuck in that mine in Chile? When my friend told me about that, I asked, "Oh, so what, they're all in high school?! What were they even doing down there?" I thought *miners* were *minors*. SO funny, I mean not that they were trapped… nevermind, I guess you had to be there.'

'We have so many threads to pull on. Where would you like to start?'

'Okay. Um, well, I kinda distanced myself from Pete again, and then, he hooked up with my best friend. Well, not my best friend but I'd call her a bestie, for sure. But I guess I slept with someone else first, so I can't really judge.'

'How do you know he had sexual relations with your friend?'

'I saw it.'

'Like it was one of your visions or you really saw it?'

'I drove to her apartment, took a key, opened the door, and walked into the bedroom where his head was between her legs, which was very fuck the patriarchy but also very fuck my life.'

'Oh. I'm sorry. That must have been upsetting.'

'Can I ask you a question now?'

'Of course.'

'How about you? How's your love life? Are you dating anyone?'

Moseby tries very, very hard to hold in their reaction. 'We're here to talk about you. How are *you* doing, Ellie? With everything?'

'My ego is LOVING the attention. Basking in it, really.'

Moseby reaches for her whistle. They put their mouth around it, about to blow.

'Okay, fine, fine. Um…'

Silence. Ellie looks to the side as her eyes begin to well up. Her emotions are coming to the surface, and she doesn't like it. Meanwhile, Moseby is delighted to have finally cracked this nut. *Literally.*

'Actually, my family has been mostly shit about this.'

'How do you mean?'

'My dad's wife is relentless. Hounding me about how horrible I am for being an unwed mother. My uncle seems to be leading the witch hunt against me to prove I'm a lunatic, all while claiming *he's* the target of a witch hunt. I don't know, it's bizarre. And I still don't know who the dad is, for sure. I keep putting off talking to Pete and I know that's only making it worse.' She starts to reign in her emotions. 'The only person I really have is Austin. And Gigi. And you, of course.'

'That's okay, really, you don't have to include me, although you are correct, you do have my full support.'

'But yeah, it's just, like, lonely, I guess? I wonder if I'm even making the right decision. Or what the right decision even is anymore.'

She pauses, knowing it's time to finally address the thing she's avoided the most, even though it hurts the worst. Moseby doesn't say a word, hoping she'll continue. And she does.

'I really can't believe this is happening without my brother. Pinky was my best friend and then, whoosh. Gone. How do I know that isn't going to happen with my baby? What if I'm really not cut out to do this?'

She can't stop the tears. They pour down her face, like a waterfall that's been dammed up for far too long.

Moseby maintains steady eye contact. 'How does your body feel? Right now?'

Ellie remembers all the feelings she's pushed down. In her car, in her bed, on a bench, everywhere she goes, actually. 'Numb. Like life hurts too much.'

Moseby thinks for a minute. 'You know, I think that's actually a healthy response to what you've been through.'

Wiping her eyes, Ellie is the one in shock for once. 'Really?'

'Life does hurt too much, sometimes. And there's nothing I can say to change that. I'm very sorry for all you've been through. Especially with your brother. And you're right, you might have an equally painful experience with your baby. Or a really healing one. The truth is we don't know what the future holds. But projecting the past onto your baby, that's not going to make anything easier. That's all we know, for sure.'

'I know, I know. I just have this thing inside me that refuses to let go, like I need to fix it before I do. And I can't fix what happened to Pinky. I can't seem to fix *anything*.'

'You're right, you can't change what happened. The only thing you can control is yourself – your choices, your responses, your words, your love. And of course, you want to fix it. You have a big heart.'

'But how do I, like, move forward? How do I know this isn't just all going to happen again?'

'You don't know. You take that love you have in that big heart of yours and you multiply it and you give it to your baby. Think of this as a second chance. You deserve that, you know.'

Moseby gets up and sits next to Ellie on the couch, because as much as they want to keep things professional, they are also a human with a beating heart, and they see her pain. They know what a brutal situation Ellie is in, and they also know that they care, more than they should. Maybe all Ellie needed was someone to reassure her, to tell her it's all going to be okay, and that's okay too. They can talk about clearing up the Savior rumors next time. It's not like the media is going to let it go anytime soon. It won't become *less* viral overnight.

Ellie shakes her head and chuckles, clearly uncomfortable by how supportive Moseby is being.

'Look at me. You're making the right choice.' And then, they say the words that Ellie has been waiting to hear this whole time, from someone other than her BFF and her grandmother, who *have* to say them.

'I believe in you. You can do this.'

That burning feeling in her throat. She can barely reply. 'Thank you.'

'How about this…I want you to think of one thing you can do this week to make your life better, right here, right now? Will you do that and take one baby step, no matter what it is?'

Ellie looks up, fingers zooming through the sand finger garden. 'Of course. Anything for you.' She starts to get up and go in for a hug. 'You're the best therapist in the whole wide-'

Moseby immediately shoots their hand up. 'Ellie, fine, I'll give my consent just this once, but do not make this a regular-'

Too late. She's already got them in a bear grip and for once, they both feel comforted by it.

35

Using her finger, Ellie intently browses the books, taking time to reflect and react to each title, like she's starring in the 'Baby One More Time' music video. And she *is* being watched. Critically. By Wendy (she/her, she thinks?), the store clerk who is a tinge gothic. She's already made her evaluation of Ellie, and it's not favorable.

Wendy has been working at the bookstore for eight years, alongside her three other jobs. Her patience for shitty privileged co-workers is in the negative at this point. She grew up in the city and can spot people like Ellie from a mile away. One of the rich Marin kids, running away from daddy's money to "find themselves" in the rugged urban jungle, with a trust fund to fall back on. Except that's actually not the case for Ellie. Generational wealth was only a privilege until she decided to live differently than the generations before.

'Are you here for the interview?'

'Yes, yes, I am. My name is Elizabeth.'

Ellie shoots out her hand, an aggressively professional hello. In the wee morning hours, she marched up Russian Hill, patrolling Union Street as she prepared for this moment. She submitted her application online last night but decided to show up the moment the doors opened, just to be safe. *If only she'd been as safe in the bedroom too…*

Wendy ignores the gesture. 'Okay, why don't you follow me to the back?'

'I'd prefer to do the interview out here, if that's okay. Back rooms and me, we don't get along. Anymore. Sorry.'

Two seconds later, Ted (he/him), the bookstore owner, appears. He is old enough to be Ellie's dad and he bought this bookstore when he quit working on Wall Street in an attempt to lower his blood pressure. He switched coasts, leaving the East for the West, but after being mocked by most of his peers and family, he created a life that doesn't give him heart palpitations, one that feels really successful to him, no matter what anyone else has to say about it. The only thing that *does* concern him, though, is avoiding a scandal that might ruin everything he's created. Like, say, accidentally hiring a stripper and being shunned by his wealthy clientele in Pacific Heights, the same people who, ironically, are also the largest client base at the dance club. *But no one can know that!!!*

'Elizabeth, nice to meet you.'

Ted reaches out his hand, which Ellie hesitantly shakes. She finds herself oddly silent, for once. To be honest, she's not sure how to be around an older man in a business setting, fully clothed. It feels...odd. So, she says as little as possible, for the first time (ever) in her life.

'Have you worked retail before?'

'You could say that.'

'I'll take that as a no. Do you know how to run a cash register?'

'Yes.'

'Have you done it before?'

'No.'

'Have you ever been arrested?'

'Not in this state.'

Ted considers her. It's clear he doesn't recognize her from the news. He registers the desperation in her eyes. And the fear. *My god, she looks so afraid.*

'Okay well, look, I can tell you're bullshitting me a little, but I need someone and you're here and you seem relatively capable, so you can start tomorrow.'

In response, his worst nightmare begins to unfold. Ellie clings to his midsection, hugging him tightly. 'Thank you, Sir. I promise you won't regret this decision.'

He holds his arms up and steps back, extending his hand for another shake. 'Prove it.'

Meanwhile, Wendy firmly plants her forehead on the bookshelf in front of her. There's currently only one person in this store who feels genuinely happy about this new hire, and that's the one being hired.

36

With all the notifications blowing up Ellie's phone, it was shocking to see Aunt Sally was the most adamant about "stepping up." She sent long, essay-style texts explaining how she could relate, what with her (one) viral dog video and all. She even came up to San Francisco, renting an all-glass Airbnb in Dolores Heights, to "be there" for Ellie. It was flattering, until Ellie sat eating take-out on her aunt's rental couch and the true motive dawned on her. *Ah yes, attention.*

Since the press conference and the first raging headlines, Ellie kept an incredibly low profile, wearing a disguise to therapy, even to her interview, praying the attention would dwindle away.

Unfortunately, it's only gotten worse. She learned (the hard way) what being "doxed" means: when strangers find and reveal your private information, like your address. Now, wherever she goes, a swarm of reporters and weird men with big lenses follow. And they're parked outside her aunt's conveniently see-through rental.

Aunt Sally won't stop peeking through the window, three to four times per minute, on average. It's quite obvious she's more excited than annoyed by the press. She even put a discrete lawn sign with her dogs' social media handle out front. *Anything for followers.*

Honestly, Ellie doesn't even care, at this point. It's just refreshing to have anyone with her DNA (besides Gigi) be nice to her. Of course, they're watching *Handsome Man*, her aunt's favorite. It's the popular show about a guy who gets picked up while working the corner by a rich business woman who transforms him into marriage material.

Aunt Sally abruptly announces mid-episode, 'You know, I was once pregnant, like you. Two times, actually, but it was complicated. I didn't have the same options you do.'

Ellie starts to respond. 'I had no idea. I'm so…sorry?'

'Oh, dear! No sorries needed. I had no doubts, I did what I had to do.'

Hesitantly, Ellie steps into the minefield. 'I thought about it, but-'

Thankfully, her aunt cuts her off. 'I want you to know you're very lucky to have *options*. But wait, there's more. I was never going to tell you this but I think it's important you know.'

Ellie nods, urging her to go on.

'I will never forget the first moment I saw you. You were only one day old. When your mom got the call from the church, we raced to pick you up.'

'Wait, what?'

'I thought your mom told you.'

'Told me what? Wait, *what* are you talking about?'

'Oh geez, okay. Well, your mom has been planning to tell you but I guess I beat her to it.'

At this point, Ellie braces herself while her aunt gets up, sits down next to her on the couch, and adjusts her angle for the cameras outside.

'Elizabeth, there's no easy way to say this. You're adopted. Father Tom arranged the whole thing for your mother. But, as you know, your brother was her favorite, of course, because he was hers.'

Ellie takes this in, knowing her aunt wants a big reaction. But honestly, she's just not in the mood. There's enough misinformation floating around about her and her future, she doesn't need any more from her past. She's had enough drama for a lifetime. Plus, the misgendering of her brother is very much on purpose. *An instant trigger.*

'Oh actually, yeah my mom *did* tell me, but she asked me not to say anything to anyone, so I guess I kinda buried it.'

'I know you've had your mental challenges, which is why I want you to consider adoption. It might not only be what's best for you, but also for the baby. There are plenty of people out there who are dying to be parents, just like your mom was.' Ellie can't help but choke on her pizza a little bit. Luckily, her aunt's grand finale is sweet. 'But I support you, no matter what you *choose.*'

Looking down at her belly, Ellie responds thoughtfully. 'I'm pretty settled on my decision, but I'll think about it. Thank you.'

'That's all I wanted.'

Aunt Sally quickly turns her attention back to the show, as if she didn't just drop a bombshell on her niece's head. Meanwhile, Ellie's phone buzzes.

GUY: Saw the news. Let's talk. This is Guy, btw. THE Guy, not just any guy ;)

Ellie ignores his message, texting Austin instead:

Aunt Sally just told me I'm adopted?!? Wtf.

On the screen, the Handsome Man is wearing a tux, spinning around for the wealthy CEO woman who saved him from the streets.

AUSTIN: Omfg, don't listen to her. You literally took a DNA test, remember? You're 100% THAT Bitch. Jk. But really, there's a new Diane Keaton movie out about adoption, that's definitely where this is coming from

AUSTIN: P.S. Respond to Guy, he's texting me to get to you and it's awkwarrrrrrrd!!!

While continuing to watch one man's beautification, Ellie decides to ignore the outside world for a bit longer, tucking her most prized possession (her phone) under the couch cushion. Maybe if she just pushes reality away for a little while, it'll leave her alone too. *It seems to work just fine for her aunt.*

37

The drive home was a nightmare. Cameras on every corner and not just the kind installed by the police-state. Ones held by men on crotch rockets, sniffing her out like jaguars. Whether she tried to get home via the Presidio, amongst the tourists at the Palace of Fine Arts, or down by the water, there was always a man with a big, strap-on lens waiting around every corner. Luckily, she was able to sneak up her back alley and rush through her back door—but even there, she's not alone.

Austin is on her couch, with what looks like their second (third?) bottle of champagne, wearing a purple wig and a skintight dress. Ellie deconditioned herself from heteronormative wardrobe standards a *long* time ago. Mostly, she lost any judgment of clothing the first time she was required to wear a G-string in front of a group of "gentlemen" who also made the rule that she should cover up in public. *I mean, the dance club was funded by men, for men, but it's the way WOMEN dress that's the problem, amiright?* She knows better than *anyone* what it feels like to live in a hypocritical matrix, defined by rigid gender "rules." She firmly believes that if Austin wants to wear a tight dress and heels with B.D.E., then that's perfect. *Preferable, actually.*

'Love the 'fit.'

Flustered, Austin pops up from the couch. 'Yeah well, we have issues. I currently do NOT feel safe, and that's not an experience I'm available for.' They turn their head up to the ceiling. 'Universe, I'm NOT manifesting this energy!'

Concerned, Ellie gets closer to them. 'What's going on? Are you okay? Did someone hurt you?'

Closing their eyes and taking a deep breath, Austin motions for her to sit down next to them. They softly pick up the remote. 'I don't want to do this to you, but I think it's important you see this so you understand the gravity of danger we're facing here. I really, sincerely, with all my heart, am begging you to move.'

With that, they press play. The headlines flash across the screen:

STRIPPER MOM HUNT: This Baby Can't Be Born!

We Won't Let a SINGLE LESBIAN Do This!

SATAN BABY: You're Not Welcome Here! Go to Mars with Elon!

THE DEATH OF DECENCY

And then, the other end of the spectrum:

We Stan a Single Mom. Yas Queen!

Did this Mom-to-Be Just Single Handedly Break the Patriarchy?

Our Savior Mom is Here and She's Slaying

THE BIRTH OF THE NEW WORLD: Every Crystal You Need to Prepare for the Second Coming

Protestors from both sides have hit the streets, in New York, Chicago, Austin, Seattle, Los Angeles, and right here in San Francisco. Even in London. Ellie watches as police around the world use batons, rubber bullets, pepper spray, and tear gas on innocent, albeit opinionated, people.

And then, she sees Austin on the screen, from earlier today, in the same outfit they're wearing now. They're pulling up to her place in one of those (tourist) go-karts people rent to see the city, pretending to be a European on holiday, but their plan clearly failed. *Miserably*. Of course, the press recognized them and they were forced to make their first statement, while running to Ellie's front door.

'Alright, fine, you want a comment?! I've been waiting my whole life to say this. You people are the taints of society. LOOK AT YOU, chasing after an innocent mother-to-be. Just back up please and understand that a young mother needs your good thoughts and most importantly, your prayers, if you believe in that so much. That is all.'

With that mic drop, Austin finally gets the front door open, to the sounds of the religious protestors screaming every vile queer-hating name under the sun behind them.

Tears roll down Ellie's face as she turns to her bestie, expecting them to melt in hurt with her. Instead, Austin is lit out of a cannon.

'Oh no, we're not crying about this. We're taking action, sweetheart. This is the 21st century, these bigots will NOT get away with this. You think I care what Timbo with the missing teeth from Tennessee thinks of me?! No way, we will not be victimized!'

Just as quickly as her tears came, they're replaced by tears of joy. She's not sure how she deserved a friend like Austin, but my goddess, she's so grateful to have them.

'Oh, let me grab the popcorn, there's more!'

With a load of spunky fury, Austin turns up the volume on the next interview, handing Ellie the giant bowl of kettle corn. A Southern woman. *This will be good.*

'You know what I can't handle? How she dares to call this bastard child the next Savior. This woman deserves a slow, terrible death.'

The reporter fires back. 'Like a crucifixion?'

'Yes, *exactly.* We don't tolerate this shit in my neck of the woods.'

The besties look at each other. They both know they shouldn't, but Ellie starts it first. It's not meant to be mean-spirited, more of a release from *all* the tension that's swirling around them.

'It's the grown-out roots for me.'

'It's the accent for me.'

'It's the fake earrings for me.'

'It's the halitosis I can smell through the screen for me.'

'It's the ill-fitting push-up bra for me.'

'It's the homophobic undertones and the implication that white women are superior, for me.'

'You win.'

'I know.' Austin pauses. 'It's your turn tomorrow. Are you ready?'

'Not really, but I don't have much of a choice at this point.'

'True. Well, we both know you're going to look gorge.'

'And you will look stunning too, my dear.'

'Oh honey, that I know. I might wear this.'

Ellie lights up, delighted. 'Please do!'

38

'Quiet! We're live in three!'

After much collective harassment, Ellie finally agreed to tell her side of the story. Mostly in hopes that speaking up would be the catalyst to end all the craziness. She might have to suffer through another week of acute madness after this, but then, everyone can *move on*! So, she finds herself seated in the hot seat at the most popular Bay Area morning show. The studio is just north of her former workplace with an absolutely exquisite view of Coit Tower. The only phallic structure Ellie admires because it's not actually phallic at all! Lillie Hitchcock Coit was wild—she was filthy rich, a voracious gambler, a sharpshooter (literally), and a successful firefighter. She even disguised herself as a man just to sneak into places where "no dames" were allowed. *In other words, a gender-bending hero.* When Lillie died, she left a whopping chunk of change to her beloved city, and her donation ended up becoming Coit Tower, a penis-inspired firehose with a statue of three firemen carrying a woman out front. *Should be Lillie carrying three men, but the patriarchy is everywhere!*

Even though Ellie's nervous, this symbol honoring a wild woman shooting towards the sky is giving her energy. And she just cannot wait to clear the air and get on with life. Since this all began, in only a few weeks, she's had lawsuits filed against her, along with a daily barrage of articles, hashtags, and stinky paparazzi on her tail. She knows *anything* she says will add fuel to the fire. But she's hoping her confession today will be like a firehose of truth to soothe the flames of hate.

Of course, Austin and Gigi are right there with her, sitting behind the camera, beyond thrilled. Gigi is keeping a close eye on production, ensuring her granddaughter is shown in a good light (literally and metaphorically) while Austin is hoping to (perchance) get "discovered."

The reporter turns to Ellie, assuring her of how this is all going to go. 'Okay so when we start, don't say anything until I address you. We're going to be showing some of the things that have been said about you first, so feel free to plug your ears. Or close your eyes. Whatever you have to do. Then, you'll have your chance to speak, sound good?'

'Yeah, I'll just wait until you ask me a question.'

Her response is not acknowledged. Ellie nervously looks at her bestie.

They see her nerves, pulsing off the set, so they scream a little too loudly, 'You're glowing!!!'

The director did not like this outburst. 'QUIET ON THE SET!'

This triggers Gigi to scream, 'You're doing great sweetie!!' *Big Kris Jenner fan.*

The director scoffs, then motions with his fingers to *3, 2, 1.* A montage of news clips starts, featuring a parade of headlines:

FAMILY VALUES ARE DEAD: Stripper claims she's carrying Savior on Christmas Eve

A CASH IN! Pregnant "Virgin" Mother set to sign sponsorship deals, all for personal gain

NEW AGE HOKEY POKEY: Why can't the Savior's mom keep her hands off her bump?

UNWED MOTHER MORNING SICKNESS CURE: Linked to drought, famine, tsunamis, wildfires, and probably, the apocalypse

SLAY QUEEN: Our New Queen Mother is Giving Cleopatra Vibes with this Look

HOLY MOTHER OF GOD: Check out this pregnant GODDESS, Gen Z's Savior

The reporter starts in, unphased by the glaring misogyny and polarity on the screen.

'For Ellie Jones, this has been quite a start to the new year. She has newfound fame and a new baby on the way, who she claims may be the Messiah, returning. Although many have felt uplifted by her proclamation, there's another story happening here too. Of the true pressures of life in the spotlight and the toll it has taken on her.'

The director gives Ellie the signal to uncover her eyes and begin the interview, as the reporter asks, 'What are your initial thoughts, after seeing all that?'

'Um, well, I'm pregnant and vulnerable and this is really challenging. I realize this is all happening because of what I said, about the Second Coming, and I'd like to address that-'

'Of course, we'll get there. But first, we need to know how you're reacting to what's being said about you, not just here, but all around the world.'

'Okay, yes, I understand the magnitude, trust me I feel it and it does not feel good. When you're pregnant, you know...well, actually I guess *you* don't know…'

The male reporter gets flustered.

Ellie continues. 'Especially being pregnant, it's just *a lot* and then you add all *this* on top of just trying to become a new mom, it's, um…'

'It sounds like a heavy burden. How are you handling it?'

'Well, thank you for asking, because most people don't, but yeah, it's just been a lot to handle. Too much.'

'Would you say that you're really...not okay? You're struggling?'

'I mean, yes, it's been hard.'

'So, you're barely getting by. Let's switch gears here for a minute.'

Gigi is shooting daggers at this guy from her chair while Austin can't stop twirling their hands.

'Is it true you're unsure of who the father is?'

'I'm not really sure why that matters.'

'Many would disagree. Paternity matters the *most*, actually.'

'Well, stay tuned, then.'

'Is it also true that you're part of the LGBTQ+ community?'

Ellie looks at her support crew, surprised. They both give her an eager thumbs up.

'Yes, but I'm not sure how that's relevant...'

'Do you think your sexual preferences are preventing you from deciding who the father is?'

'What are you implying?'

'Would you make the same choice of keeping the father's identity a secret if you weren't a queer? I know you were born this way, but would you choose for your baby to be born like *that*, too?'

Ellie takes a long deep sigh. Gigi has been preparing her for this her whole life. Now is her moment to shine.

'*Sir*, first of all, I wasn't "born this way"—I'm queer because I want to be. My sexuality is something I'd choose over and over again, every time. Can you stop treating it like it's some genetic flaw? Secondly, I hope you understand that sexuality and gender identity are much more nuanced than two binary choices. The only reason bodies have been grouped together into two categories is for socioeconomic purposes. You get that, right?'

'Please watch your tone. This is a *family* show. And I'll be the one asking questions here. So, you don't believe your baby needs a father?'

'My baby has a loving parent and support from a chosen family who cares, and that's all that matters.'

'Are you saying this baby, who let me remind you, you claim is the *Savior*, could potentially have *no* father at all?! Or worse, *only* a mother?'

Austin bites their nails. Gigi grins from ear to ear. They both know Ellie is two seconds away from letting her Scorpio stinger annihilate this guy, which would be fine in any other circumstance, but right now, she needs to clear up the rumors.

Not knowing which direction this will go, Austin starts sending long distance reiki in Ellie's direction, hoping that the online webinar they took on energy healing will pay off. Gigi simply sits back and relishes in the moment. She's never been prouder of her granddaughter, and it shows.

'Look, I'm not sure why you are so *obsessed* with who sleeps in my bed. This honestly feels like a personal issue for *you*, one that I recommend you sort out with a therapist, sooner than later. Obviously, being who I am, comes with a level of judgment and harassment, even danger, but I love who I am and I love my baby and that's all you and the world need to know.'

She touches her bump and it's clear she's angry and flustered, which has caused her to lose track of her original motive for being here in the first place. She quickly took up the cause of the girls and the gays, because she's had to defend herself in this world where blatant prejudice is somehow the social norm. The reporter is acting as if he's in stunned silence, but purposefully lets her continue, knowing this is clickbait gold.

She goes on. 'The way you're asking me about my sexuality, you're insinuating that being *not* straight is somehow inferior to being heterosexual and it's just, not. If anything, I believe homosexuality is superior. There, I said it. And as for your concerns about the father, I can promise you this baby is going to be very loved and very well cared for.'

Austin pumps their fists off-screen, thinking the reiki must have worked. Gigi is glowing now too. Ellie is nailing this, even if she's forgotten to mention the whole "it's not really the Savior" part. The reporter knows this interview will be career-defining, maybe even getting him a promotion. He launches another hard-hitting question.

'Do you know the gender of the baby?'

'No, and none of us will. I don't think it's right to jam rigid gender identities onto a newborn. Call me weird!'

'Well, it has to be one or the other? A boy or girl?'

'Does it?'

'Yes, that's just the way it works. I'd advise you to be clear about this, don't make things worse for yourself.'

'You know, *Sir*, you seem *really* good at mansplaining and giving advice; how are you at *taking* it?'

'Answer the question. Do you know the gender of the baby?'

'Are you asking what kind of genitalia my fetus has? That's very creepy, especially coming from a man like you, in a position of power.'

He's losing it. 'No, like I said, I'm asking if you're having a boy or a girl.'

'I believe in gender variance.'

'That sounds like some zillennial bullcrap if I've ever heard it.' His anger is beginning to show as he doubles down. 'Do you believe in family values?'

'I think the better question is: Why do "family values" include the need to know what private parts are going to be in my child's diaper? Why are you so obsessed with the sexual organs of babies?'

The reporter turns away from her, addressing the camera and abruptly ending the conversation, while Austin and Gigi can't help but burst into applause.

'You heard it here first, folks. The fatherless, genderless Savior is on the way. We'll be right back with more, where we'll be discussing why this *charming* mother-to-be might be banned from entering a church, ever again. Stay tuned.'

As soon as they cut to commercial, Ellie hops off the soundstage and exits the studio, surrounded by the love of her people. She's not participating in another second of this bullshit. She said what she needed to say, for now.

39

'I always said a coach house would be perfect for you.'

It's no shock that the first security breach was family. So far, the media haven't even found Ellie and Austin's new address, but somehow Melanie Margaret did. She's obsessed with real estate, square footage, and most of all, with equity—so she claims she just "happened to be driving by" when she pulled up tires blazing.

Ellie immediately knew an inquisition was coming. 'I hate to disappoint you, but we're actually living in this whole house, right here.' She gestures to the 5-bed/3-bath mansion behind her.

Melanie laughs with her whole spirit. 'That's impossible.'

Austin claps back with their whole soul. 'No, actually, it's true. And please don't share the address with anyone, we had to do this for our safety. Actually, we're going to need you to sign an NDA.'

'How could this *possibly* happen? From all your silly little stomach videos?'

Even though social media has nearly ruined Ellie's world, Austin kept their accounts active, raking in millions of followers, in record time. When a "wellness" company sent a DM with a seven-figure offer, they found themselves strapped to an ab machine within hours, beer in hand, reciting the script:

'Hold up, you guys are probably wondering what I have on? This is my secret to fab abs. The best part: I can get an ab workout anytime, anywhere. Not that I need it! Kidding, this is how I got these abs. This machine did it. It's an amazing deal, get it before it expires. Link in my bio.'

If you'd told Austin one year ago they'd be flexing their abs for the masses, they would have popped off on how they'd never sell out and contribute to the consumerist, distorted wellness culture of America. But they also never would have predicted the predicament they found themselves in with Ellie: living as two openly queer people, with the attention of the world following them everywhere they went – and *no* security. The only way to stay safe was to sign whatever deals they could and pray for a miracle, some kind of savior to give them shelter and protection. *Ironic.*

Melanie is so flustered. 'How much did this cost? What's the market value? Whose name is on the mortgage? Did you guys even consider *any* of that?'

It actually happened out of nowhere, in the middle of the night. A life-changing DM, from a verified, tremendously popular musician, someone they'd listened to since they were baby queers, in their *My Humps* era:

Hey loves, want to support you. Use my place for as long as you'd like, no strings attached. My team will be in touch. xoxo P.S. Please don't tell anyone about this arrangement, want to keep my house off the Celebrity Star tours. Thanks, doll.

When Austin connected with "the team," it became clear that not only did this artist generously offer their place - a.k.a. *mansion* in Seacliff - but also, full protection from round-the-clock, 24/7 security.

People use words like "exclusive" and "elite" to describe Seacliff. Mostly because the celebrities and techies who have made their homes here, did so because of the privacy and security—two things Ellie and Austin need now too.

Their wonderful, anonymous supporter did what they could after seeing how these two were being processed through the media meat grinder. They might have been able to skirt the paparazzi for now, but it's clear that skirting Ellie's family is a whole other thing.

Melanie continues. 'Is this from all that Tic Tac stuff!? How is this legal?'

Austin lights up. 'Are you referring to the breath mint from the 80s? Because no, it's not from that.' They turn to Ellie. 'Whatever happened to those, by the way? Has anyone seen them? Where did they go? Let's invest and make the Tic Tac great again!'

As her face turns beet red, Melanie *still* cannot comprehend what's happening. 'So, you're renting then?'

Ellie finally responds. 'You know, I really don't like to talk about that kinda stuff. But rest assured, we've got it covered.' *A boundaries win. Must add to brag list for therapy.*

'Alright well, just know your father and I will *not* be bailing you out of this colossal financial mistake you're making.'

Austin takes one for the team. 'Thank you so much for your opinion. This is actually a hate-free zone, so if you could hold those thoughts to yourself, that would be wonderful.'

With that, Melanie shoves a gift in Ellie's direction and turns on her heels.

Austin can't help but scream after her. 'K, thanks hun! Appreciate you!'

* * *

As the sun sets, the soul sisters sit around the kitchen table, sipping on Ellie's favorite, absolutely delicious Ghirardelli hot chocolate. The floor-to-ceiling windows show off iconic views of the Golden Gate, along with the opening to the San Francisco Bay, the place where the water meets the Pacific Ocean.

Even though they have this place on loan, it's going to take time to adjust to this sharp twist in the wheel of fortune. Almost as if the universe said: *Look, I know this has all been brutal, but here, you'll be epicly taken care of in the process.*

After taking a long sip, Austin says something they instantly regret. 'This cocoa always reminds me of Pinky.'

Like an uncontrollable trauma response, Ellie winces a bit at the mention of her brother's name. 'Yeah, it does.'

Quickly changing the subject, Austin gestures towards the gift from the stepmonster. 'Shall we?'

Relieved to switch gears, Ellie eagerly starts the unboxing. 'What have we here?' She pulls out a T-shirt, unfolding it to reveal the text on the front:

I lost all the baby weight in only 6 weeks but who's counting?

Austin bursts out laughing. 'Did she Google "worst gifts to get a pregnant woman?" There's so many layers to this. The fat-shaming. The misogyny. I can't.'

Ellie is not amused. In most circumstances, she would brush this off, finding it funny. If her brother were here, they would laugh about it. But it just feels depressing without them. Dealing with her family's dysfunction right now, with all the other hate swirling around her, it's too heavy. Like the humor has been sucked out and replaced with what's underneath: pain. It feels like no matter how hard she tries, her family will always have these little flying monkeys, tracking her down, reminding her of how much they value her (*not much*) and how much they disapprove of her lifestyle (*very much*).

'Why is she always so fucking passive aggressive? Like what did I ever do to her, actually? Besides just exist.'

As she gets up from the table and marches down the long, marble hallway, she feels it. She sprints through the bathroom door, finding herself in a familiar position: sitting on the toilet, waiting to see the status of her pregnancy. Only this time, she sees blood.

40

'Can you please step on it a little?'

Bertha moves at the pace of an original trolley car down the side roads.

'This is as fast as I can go. The signs clearly state the speed limit, and you know I get anxiety while driving on hills, this is the best I can do. What's your blood loss looking like? A quart? A gallon?'

Austin's complexion has a hint of green and it's not from using a color-correcting concealer stick. Other than hill driving, they are also terrified of blood, needles, and vaginas. So, to their defense, this situation is the culmination of all their worst fears, molded into one. And Ellie knows that.

'Deary, it's okay. It's only a tiny bit but I just want to get checked out. We could walk...would that be better?'

'No, no, no, no. no, if I'm going to be a *central* parental figure in this child's life, then I need to learn to STEP IT UP. I've got this.'

At a slow but steady pace, Bertha creeps up Pine Street, much like a turtle, even though the passengers both currently have the energy of a hare.

Miraculously, they arrive at UCSF hospital in under an hour, mostly because Ellie (gently) cattle prodded Austin (and Bertha) the entire way. And now, they wait because the American healthcare system is so... efficient. Especially in the middle of a weekend night in a big city. Just a short five- to seven-hour wait. *No big deal.*

On the exam table, Ellie shivers under the paper sheets. Meanwhile, standing at her side, Austin examines the stir-ups, needing something to disperse their anxious energy on to. They pull them in and out, in and out, in and out, playing around, scrutinizing every intricacy of how they work.

'You know what? I think these could be super profitable for home use. I know I'd love a pair for my bed. They're kinda cute and could be pretty fun, don't you think?!'

Abruptly, the doctor, a near-the-end-of-his-career man who prefers to be taken seriously, enters, like he was actively trying to spook them.

Austin screeches, fumbling to put the stir-ups back into their proper place. 'Sorry, sorry. Hello there!'

The doctor is not amused. 'You're the father?'

'No, no. More of a fairy godmother type presence.'

Ellie tries to get the doctor's attention. 'I'm the mother.'

'I know.' The doctor turns his back to look at the chart. 'Marital status?'

'How is that relevant?'

'Date of last period?'

'Um, obviously not for a while. But I am spotting. That's why I'm here.'

'Age?'

'33.'

Austin interjects. 'Her Jesus year!'

'So, geriatric.'

Once again, Austin can't help but insert their commentary. 'Geriatric?! We're still doing ageism? At *your* big age?!'

Ellie swats the air towards them, signaling a call for silence. This is not the time for advocacy, as much as she agrees. The doctor goes about his business and starts lubing up Ellie's stomach for the ultrasound.

As he moves the wand around and around, there's not a sound from anyone or anything. Austin squeezes Ellie's hand, trying to look hopeful while doing a terrible job of hiding their true concern.

The doctor finally speaks. 'I'm not getting a heartbeat. Hang on.'

He leaves the room. The besties can't even look at each other. Ellie has her eyes closed, trying to stay calm. Austin has their eyes closed, visualizing the most expansive outcome of this moment. After a long, painfully drawn-out silence, the doctor comes back, wheeling in a new cart. He plugs it in and places the ultrasound wand on Ellie's belly.

'Oh, there we go. That one must be faulty.' He screams outside the door. 'Janet, we need to ditch machine #237. It's defective.'

Within three seconds, the heartbeat comes through, loud and clear. Austin fans themself, making an expectedly dramatic exhalation, hugging Ellie profusely. She has finally opened her eyes, letting out a single tear, as she looks at the monitor with pure wonder and awe, wishing she could bring this (working) machine home with her, so she could watch her baby every minute of every day, ensuring nothing bad will ever happen to them.

Finally, Doctor Friendly turns to Ellie. 'Everything looks good and your baby is healthy. A little spotting is normal from time to time, and is usually a sign of distress in the mother.' He proceeds to lecture her on limiting stress, as if that's remotely possible with the shitstorm surrounding her. *She'll do her best but can make no promises. Have you seen the headlines, Sir?!*

Austin can't help but interject. 'Oh, okay, yeah, yeah, we'll do that. But with bigotry, climate change, inflation, classism, and clickbait media, it's not the easiest task. Maybe we can live in a bubble?'

Dryly, the doctor responds. 'I wouldn't advise it. But whatever you need to do.'

41

The next morning, bright & early, Ellie is parked on a steep uphill slant. She checks Bertha's emergency brake like five times, knowing she will forget that it's on. She's becoming more aware of her patterns. *Something else to brag about to Moseby.*

Regardless of the drama with the parking brake, Ellie's determined to take action to create a more peaceful, stable environment for her growing baby. She spots who she's been waiting for, walking up the street, and immediately jumps out of the car.

'Hi, um, it's me, Ellie.'

'I know who you are.'

'Can we talk?'

'Do I have a choice?'

Ted opens the door to the store, letting her enter first. Facing off awkwardly on either side of the register, they're both unsure of the vibe between them. Determined to complete her mission, Ellie leads the charge.

'Look, Edward. Or Theodore. Simon, Edward, Theodore! Remember that?'

'Please, just call me Ted.'

'Isn't it weird how Ted is short for Edward *and* Theodore though? I mean, you've probably been dealing with that your whole life but it still boggles my mind.'

'Did you come here to talk about *The Chipmunks* or what, exactly…'

'Right. Look, I'm really, really sorry about what I did. Honestly, I thought it was something special and unique but I did not ask for consent and that's not okay with ME. However, I think we can both admit the store looked really cute, like a whole new vibe, especially when this whole section over here was all red. But I now understand why the books are organized by *author*, not by *color*. Although, you do have to admit, the color blocking was great for socials.'

'Not great for inventory though. Or finding a book, the whole point of this store.'

'You're absolutely correct. I am truly, very sorry, from the bottom of my heart. It was never my intention to cause any trouble. However, I do know the difference between intention and impact so again, I'm sorry.'

Ted was not pleased then, and he still isn't now. 'I have a feeling you're not just here to apologize, so let's cut to the chase.'

'You're right. Has anyone ever told you how smart you are?'

Ted will not be buttered.

'Okay, truth. I was hoping you would put me back on the schedule.'

'You know, if we're going to be truthful, then you need to know that I took a chance on you, and you blew it. I can't do that again, this place is my livelihood. Do you understand that?'

As if on cue, a scruffy photographer starts taking pictures through the window, leading Ted to dodge behind the register.

'And now you're bringing all your drama into my store. No way. Sorry, you need to go. Now.'

For once, Ellie has nothing to say. She just starts tearing up as more and more pictures are taken.

'Oh god. Okay, just please, okay, no.' Ted ushers her away from the window, towards the back of the store.

He cannot get this kind of publicity. Lord knows what the Internet will say about a pregnant woman crying alone with a man of his age. He'll probably be accused of being the father! *A career-ender.* So, he just lets her talk, anything to keep her away from the windows.

'Fine, look, you're right, I'm really sorry. I'm just in a tight spot right now and I don't follow directions well but I don't know what else to do. My whole life feels like one colossal mistake after the next, I don't know how to stop making them, it's the only thing I'm good at and no one will hire me for that, so here I am.'

Ted pauses, considering her. 'Wait here.'

He curtly walks to the register and opens a drawer, picking something up and marching right back. He's unsure if he's doing this out of genuine empathy or self-preservation. Either way, it's the only viable option he has right now. He hands her back her name tag.

Ellie's tears softly begin to dry up as she looks up at him. 'I promise you won't regret this.'

'I sure hope not. Just please use the back door when you come and go.'

Smiling from ear to ear, Ellie delightfully responds, 'That's what he-'

'Too far. No.'

* * *

MEET PETE PEREZ: the"maybe" Baby Daddy of the Second Coming

Ellie Jones is going to give birth to the Second Coming. But the world wants to know: who is the dad?

The 33-year-old mother-to-be has so far refused to identify the paternity of the baby she claims will be the next Savior. According to a reliable source, Jones has been romantically linked to Pete Perez on and off for several years—and he is now one of many potential fathers.

But who is Pete Perez, 38, her potential baby daddy, and why is he not her husband yet?

Perez grew up in the East Bay before heading to Georgetown University on a full scholarship. There, he started an internship with the U.S. government, where he continues to work to this day. His role is classified and the government refuses to comment.

Perez reportedly met Jones at a social gathering in Oakland and they've been dating ever since. They struck up a conversation, exchanged numbers, and the rest is history.

With no social media presence, it's hard to know much about Perez. According to a reliable source, he was actually looking forward to a "normal" relationship with Jones. He had plans to propose to her and has been ready to take the next step in the relationship, but Jones has turned him down, repeatedly.

Meanwhile, the mom-to-be has told the world that the identity of the father "doesn't matter." Does Pete feel the same? We highly doubt it.

COMMENTS

BABYBAE: Can someone please explain this Second Coming situation to me like I'm five?

KARENWITHAK: Having a baby daddy is so immature.

SECONDCOMINGSTAN: Pete Perez is not the real baby daddy, it's Guy Parker, owner of that bomb cookie shop.

42

'The normies are arriving at an alarming speed! Brace yourselves!'

It's clear Austin has not slept in days, surviving solely on a diet of vodka and cortisol. They have been planning this day their whole life. The guest list isn't exactly what they imagined but it's turned out better than expected, mostly because of the location. They managed to pull a few strings and secure the entire second floor of Zuni, Ellie's favorite brunch spot.

The past 48 hours have been a whirlwind of stress and dressing up the venue to the nines (in carefully curated gender-neutral baby decor, of course). *The Chronicle* is doing an exclusive on this event, which will make or break Austin's future career. This could be their golden ticket to a life of fulfilling work (especially since selling ab machines has gotten old, quick).

The guests start piling through the door and to Austin's delight (and Ellie's dismay), everyone shows up! Miserae (in all black), Daniel (in a trench coat), Maisie (plus, girlfriend), Mr. Jones (in a DASHING vintage suit), Aunt Sally (and her "only" dog), Wendy (the punk clerk), Ted (the one and only boss Ellie's ever semi-impressed) and even Moseby (against usual protocol but what in Ellie's life *is* usual?).

Austin eagerly leads everyone to the first activity: gift opening. Even three sheets to the wind, they still manage to hold it all together. So, she (kinda) does too. She sits in the (throne) chair and opens the gifts, one by one, for the audience, all so her bestie can host this prima event to kick-start their well-deserved event planning business.

'This one is from Daniel. A baby trench coat! Thank you, how sweet!'

Daniel announces to the group. 'I want to bring back the trench. Make it cool again.'

Austin pats his arm while they slam their ninth mimosa. 'Bless your heart.'

Ellie holds it up for everyone to see. 'Cheers mate! Buzzin' about this!'

Austin can't hide their buzz. 'Would anyone else like some punch?'

Gigi is the only person who responds. 'YES! I mean, sure, I'll take some.'

As Austin rushes to top off drinks, they survey the guests like a cheetah hunting a gazelle. Everything is going to plan, except for Mr. Jones and Ted. Even though Austin intended for them to become friends (as the only two cis males in the room), they seem to want *nothing* to do with each other, repelled from one another like magnets. But everyone else seems to be doing well, especially Aunt Sally. She's having a grand old time seated next to Wendy, filling her in on her pup's latest health issues, in copious detail. Until she peers out the window and her paranoia kicks in.

'Who is *that*? Out front?'

Ellie immediately responds. 'Probably just some tossers mugging me off.'

Austin swiftly closes the drapes, slurring a bit. 'Oh, down't mindth them. Just the local MOB. They're demanding to know who the father is and apparently, I'M NOT GOOD ENOUGH.'

The protestors have been gathering outside (along with the paparazzi) practically blocking Market Street with signs that read:

All Babies Deserve a Dad

Fatherless Children Are Gross!

No Daddy = Baddie (Not the Good Kind)

To top it off, they're (loudly) chanting. 'Hey, hey, ho, ho, where's the dad or to hell you'll go.'

Aunt Sally chimes in, and it's unclear if she's being ironic. 'They *are* precious. Just precious.'

Gigi rolls her eyes. 'If only these were the good old days. I'd be out there in counterprotest with a fire hose, burning my bra.'

Meanwhile, Austin is determined to stick to the schedule, even if they don't remember what it is, exactly. 'Okay, everyone, we're going to begin our first game. NOW!'

Begrudgingly and with no enthusiasm whatsoever, everyone in the party tries to ignore this, so Ellie takes this as her cue to go to the bathroom, where she's immediately confronted by the hostess, a.k.a. her party planning bestie.

'Hey dear, make it quick, okay? And can we put a hard stop on the *Love Island* chat for now, love?'

'Don't be a wanker.'

'Well, if you insist on talking British all day, then I'm just *chuffed* about how this is going.'

'Straight buzzin', like!'

Uh oh. Bloody hell.

* * *

As she washes her hands in the bathroom sink, Ellie can hear the faint cries from outside. Her phone buzzes. *Why is she always getting messages in the bathroom?*

GUY: Hey, I've been out of the country, long story. We REALLY need to talk. When can we do that, cutie?

Like déjà vu from Christmas Eve, there's a knock on the door. Only this time, it's a gentle, sweet one.

'Hey Grammy, we need you!'

'Be right out!'

Ellie looks in the mirror, in her own eyes, confident for the first time that she's got this, no matter who the dad is, no matter how many people gather outside with protest signs, no matter how many clickbait titles exist, no matter what anyone else says. *She has everything under control.*

Another knock.

'I'd fancy one more minute please!'

A timid voice replies. 'Can I come in?'

Shocked, Ellie opens the door to find Miserae. 'Are you pulling me for a chat?'

Miserae brushes past her, entering the bathroom. 'If that means I want to talk with you in private, then yes.'

Ellie shuts the door. 'It's a bit muggy to be hiding from everyone.'

'I'm not concerned about that. Are you okay?'

'I'm just knackered, that's all.'

'Why are you talking like you're from the Geordie Shore?'

'I love that show! Let's get mortal, like!'

'No one is getting mortal. I mean, other than your bestie. They are on another level.'

Ellie goes to make a joke back but sees the genuine concern in Miserae's eyes. And there's something about the way she *actually* cares that touches something in her. But quickly, she deflects.

'Wait, has hell frozen over? I can't believe you're asking me about my feelings.'

'I'm trying to be better about that. And I care about you, Ellie. This is all...*a lot.*'

Ellie decides to rip off the band-aid. 'Look, I know you've had a little thing for me, it's fine. It's great you finally decided to shoot your shot. I'm proud of you, really.'

Miserae is not amused. 'Oh, please. Don't flatter yourself.'

'It's okay, nothing to be embarrassed by, happens all the time, really. Everyone's always grafting over me, I'm used to it.'

'Ellie, I mean, yes, I like you as a person, don't get me wrong, but you're not really my type. I thought *you* were the one who had a thing for me.'

'Wow, so I'm being pied off at me own baby shower!'

Miserae ignores the (heavy) return of the British slang. 'What made you think that I had feelings for you…like that?'

'All the vibes and the chat and wanting to crack on all the time.'

'First of all, you're all over the news and every social media platform. I cannot go on the Internet without seeing your face. So, of course I wanted to see how you're doing. And it wasn't all the time. We made plans. Once. And you canceled and now I'm here. Honestly, my therapist made me come. It's part of making new connections. Fostering "healthy" friendships.'

Now Ellie really is slightly offended. 'Why are you being so salty with me?'

'I'm not. I just want to make sure you're okay.'

Ellie touches up her make-up in the mirror, so Miserae continues.

'So, is the dad involved? I didn't see him out there. I won't say anything to anyone, I promise. I can sign an NDA if you want.'

'I have two paternity options and I'm only in active communication with one of them, at the moment.'

'I'm sure it'll all work out, Ellie. What about that waiter out there? I saw you looking at him…'

'Oh him? No, no, I mean, we just know each other from a past life. Two past lives, really. I used to come here all the time for brunch and we slept together once upon a time. But in a *real* past life, I used to be a servant in a small village in Italy in the 1700s, and he was an opossum who haunted my hut. It's all very karmic. He still kinda has night rodent energy, don't you think?'

Miserae can't help but smile. 'You stopped talking like you grew up in Essex.'

Ellie finally pauses. 'Look, I slip into British mode because it reminds me of my brother, okay? We binged all of *Love Island* together. Twice. And I guess you'd probably call it a coping mechanism because I just wish they could be here for stuff like this.'

Miserae breaks her rule of no physical affection and gives Ellie a hug— one she realizes she needed.

'You are proper mint at giving hugs. I knew you were a worldie.'

'Ellie. No.'

Back in the main room, chaos has broken out. Austin planned a "secret" and had all the guests "surprise" Ellie by blowing confetti in her face as she walked back through the party, like the Olympics opening ceremony, announcing the first competition.

As she takes a seat back on the throne chair, Austin, once again, tries to wrangle everyone's attention. 'Okay, we're going to start the first game, FOR REAL NOW. I'm going to need you all to-'

With that, everyone's jaws drop to the ground as they each notice a different, unplanned surprise. A late, uninvited guest, stomping up the stairs.

'Don't mind me.'

Everyone in the room is too stunned to speak as Melanie Margaret wedges her way through the party. They also know what's coming next. Ellie had only *one* requirement with explicit instructions: no snitches. Both her maternal figures have been giving interviews, selling stories to the press, which shouldn't have been shocking, but still hurt Ellie a lot.

Austin sashays over to their bestie's "bonus" mom. 'Mrs. Jones the Second, apologies, this might be a faux pas, but I literally memorized the guest list and I can most certainly ensure you were *not* on it.'

Everyone and their mother saw the tell-all interview Ellie's stepmother gave a few weeks ago, the one where she told the reporter, 'I'm worried this child might not be Christ re-born, but the opposite.' It didn't sit well with anyone with a heart, to say the least.

Melanie Margaret tightly crosses her arms over her chest, digging her heels into the ground. 'I thought you were all about being inclusive. Now you're going to kick me out? Of my own *step*-grandchild's shower?"

With that, Father Tom pops his head up at the top of the stairs, making an even more shocking grand entrance. 'Sorry, I had to find parking.'

The truth is he tried to park on a trolley rail, an interesting choice but not surprising given his edible dosage for the day. *Could have been electrifying, though.* As he hopped out of the car, the protestors swarmed him, so happy to see their Father join in the cause, only to have all their abandonment issues triggered as they watched him join the party of blasphemy.

Austin has had enough. They are really good at keeping their temper in check, until they aren't. It's time to go off-script.

'Okay, Boomers. I don't mean to be patronizing here, but there's a lot of contradictions happening.' They turn to Melanie. 'Like you're here, but you said the baby might be the devil, so…talk to me.'

'I didn't say that. I said there was a *rumor* the child *might* be the anti-Christ. But fine, you're right, Austin. I'm the worst person in the world. Why am I even here?'

'Great question!' Austin turns back to the party, all of whom have not taken their eyes off this Scene. The only person who has made any movement at all is Gigi, who slid right next to Ellie's side, holding her hand.

Another movement stirs at the top of the stairs as Sue enters, behind Father Tom. Ellie's mom stands her ground. 'I was invited to this event, with a guest.'

Flabbergasted, Austin loudly retorts. 'Sorry Susan, but that's a lie.'

Father Tom puts his arm around his "friend." 'Lying is very bad, it's not biblical. We would never do that.'

'But you're all spreading lies! About your future grandchild. And your daughter. So why are you here?'

Sue doubles down. 'I worry about this child.'

That's it. Austin is done. 'Okay, I've held my tongue and I didn't want to create a scene…' Everyone in the room exchanges looks. 'But you've left me with no choice.' Without thinking, they flip a nearby table over in one swoop, allowing the precious decor they made with their own two hands to fall to the ground, like hail. Dramatically, they turn around like a detective mid-interrogation.

'Where were *you three* on January 6th, huh?! I'd love to know!! And so would the FBI. I think it's time to go.'

As Sue, her lover, and her ex's lover make their way towards the stairs, just as they reach the top, the stepmonster turns back. 'You're all going to hell.'

Austin finishes chugging the two champagne glasses on the nearby table, and then screams. 'Cool, BYE BITCH!'

After they take a moment for some self-reiki around the heart, they nonchalantly attempt to pick up from where they left off. 'Okay, excuse whatever *that* was, now it's time to line up for wheel-barrow races! I call bottom!'

Breaking her silence, Gigi yells, 'We know!'

43

As one might expect, the rest of the evening went downhill quicker than a tourist on roller skates descending from Coit Tower. Austin made an Irish exit, escaping off to the (conveniently nearby) Castro to meet up with the person they've been seeing. More power to them, just not ideal timing. Even though Ellie wants to feel pissed that she's left to cleanup, she doesn't. In her heart of hearts, she knows Austin deserves a break. The past few months have been like walking through a minefield for both of them. Naturally, her bestie needs to blow off some steam, especially with the quantity of uppers currently coursing through their veins.

The shower was beautifully done, with only the finest decor and just a hint of camp. Tasteful yet cheeky. *Just how they both like it.* Except now that everyone's left, Ellie is left alone to load the gifts into Bertha while Gigi runs security, making sure the "congregation" out front does indeed follow Father Tom to the closest church for the group prayer circle he promised. Probably where they'll all pray the gay away. *Whatever they're into.*

Ellie's phone buzzes.

GIGI: All clear, Grammy. So proud of you today and always. Have to ske-daddle but just know: I'm the luckiest grandma in the world to have you as a my grandperson (new term I'm trying out). Remember, all you need is love!!!

Uh oh. Whenever Gigi sends her Beatles references, she's got something up her sleeve. Ellie looks right and left as she heads out into the back alley with the last round of packages. Just as she's carefully squeezing them into the backseat, she spots a figure approaching Bertha. Without a second thought, she screams:

'I have pepper spray and I will use it!'

And then, she hears his voice. 'You don't need it.'

She feels a wave of calm wash over her whole body, even though she is also furious to learn the identity of this shadowy figure. But at least she knows she's not going to die here.

'I was really hoping I'd find you here.'

'Well, you did. Sorry I haven't…you know.'

Like most things that matter, Ellie has been delaying talking to Pete…
for weeks. The more time that went by, the more awkward it became.
And the less motivated she became to do anything about it. She wasn't
even really *that* mad about the "cheating" thing because they weren't
officially together. Plus, she can't judge. They're both human and
monogamy is a choice, one they hadn't made (at that time). So, instead
of facing the issue, she avoided it and him. Reasoning with herself that
by *not* talking to Pete, she was actually saving him a world of pain.
Letting him avoid this whole mess. Really, the opposite was true.

'Will you please talk to me, Ellie? I promise, I come in peace.'

'How did you know I was here?'

'The whole world knows where you are. I can't go on my phone
without seeing your face.'

'I guess I am pretty popular these days.'

Grinning, he retorts. 'Please don't tell me you've become a diva now.'

'We all change, Pete. Not to be a high maintenance celeb, but can we
maybe have this discussion over, say, food? I'm fucking starving.'

Immediately, Pete agrees and also insists on driving Bertha. Not in a
patriarchy way, in a protecting the baby and Ellie's energy way, which
she finds endearing. He's racking up points right and left, but it doesn't
matter because there's no reason to keep score.

Ellie knows the only way Pete was (really) able to find her was through
Gigi. Her grandmother has always been a big fan of him (the one male
she deems "unproblematic"). She's encouraged Ellie to "stay on good
terms" because "life is long and love is rare." But it's really hard for
Ellie to do that. Mostly because she's terrified of losing someone she
loves, again.

Luckily, Mel's Drive-In is fairly empty. The dinner rush has passed and

most tourists are cranky from the time change and spending hours
illegally feeding seals down at Fisherman's Wharf. Ellie and Pete have
the place pretty much to themselves, which feels sweet. *Romantic, even.*

Pete has been bringing Ellie here since they first met and they both
always get the same thing. Mozzarella sticks and a milkshake for her, a
Smash Burger and an Arnold Palmer for him. Not the most organic
options, but they have bigger things to worry about. And right now,
Ellie's hangry—and they both know it.

Pete tries to warm her up. 'How have you been?'

'Fine. Good.'

He runs his fingers through his hair and leans back. It's clear this isn't
going to be easy. He reconsiders. 'Look, I'm so sorry Ellie. I really
fucked up.'

'Oh, you think? Wow, thank you. What a revelation.'

'I mean it, I'm really sorry. And I'm so sorry you've been going through
all this, alone.'

'I haven't been alone. The people who love me have been right by my
side.'

Like manna from heaven, the food arrives. They eat in silence, as Pete
eagerly waits for the mozz sticks to enter Ellie's digestive track, moving
her into a more satiated mode.

As she takes one last bite of a cheese stick, she scoots out of the booth.
'Okay, well, thanks.'

Pete holds her arm and she looks down at it. The spark that runs
between them feels like the two fingers on the Sistine Chapel finally
touching, after all these centuries. Compelled by a force much greater
than her stubborn will, Ellie sits back down.

He motions towards her plate. 'Can I finish those?'

She nods. He eats the rest of her mozz sticks, even though he's lactose intolerant. That's one of the many things Ellie loves about him. He lives on the edge for her, pushing the boundaries of what he thought his life would be, and instead, embracing what it could be, even if the consequences aren't always easy. *In life or the bathroom.*

'Ellie, I have a few things to say so just let me say them, please.'

She nods, sincerely, without an ounce of anything but openness.

'Look, obviously, I had no idea you were pregnant until I saw it *on the news*, but I'm really, really sorry Ellie. Things with us have been so up and down, and I'm not making any excuses, I own what I did but I want you to understand, it was like self-sabotage or something. I think I did it because I could see I wasn't making you happy and that made me unhappy, so I figured, like subconsciously, if I just did something, then it would end, right? But I was wrong. Really wrong. I've thought for a long time about why you keep pushing me away.'

The tears come and she doesn't stop them.

'I know we have to talk about the baby, and I just don't want you to feel any pressure, you have enough of that right now. I'm assuming it might be mine, but then again, it might not be, so either way, I want you to know it doesn't matter because I want to be in your life and the baby's life, however you want me to be. And I don't know if I'll ever be enough for you, but all I can do is try, okay?'

Ellie gets up and slides next to him in the booth, putting her head on his shoulder. If there's anything Ellie's learned, it's that a person is not the mistakes they've made. She's made plenty to understand that some-times, we just fuck up and that's okay. What matters is the people who are willing to work through it, the people who are willing to stay.

44

'Bit sad innit.'

That's what she said when she found out. Four words, condensed into three. Making a joke, even during the worst moment of her life. Because at that point, life felt like a joke. *A really cruel one.*

Paul was her brother's birth name, but Pinky always fit better. Her mom used to dress them both in matching Laura Ashley outfits, so really, no one should have been *too* shocked when Paul became Pinky.

Even after the change, they still decided to call each other brother and sister, mostly because they loved the yin and the yang of it. They really were the bread to each other's butter.

When Pinky was Paul, they were the apple of Sue's eye. They (he, according to their mom) could do no wrong, whereas Ellie could *only* do wrong. Somehow, despite the obvious wedge placed between the two siblings, they still managed to be close. *Like twins still in utero, close.*

As the oldest, Pinky was fiercely protective of Ellie, and as the youngest, she loved the feeling of being looked after. They taught her how to swim, how to walk, how to dance, and how to read. When they caught some little boys teasing Ellie on the playground, they marched right up, at only four feet tall, and screamed, 'If you want to start some shit, we can start some shit!' It was at that moment that Ellie felt she'd always be protected in this world.

With all the turmoil in their home life, being together felt like the only relief, outside of when Gigi would visit. Or when Austin was around. Pinky saw it all, everything that happened behind closed doors, the things Gigi and Austin would never get to see. And Ellie saw what Pinky had to go through with their dad. A man who hated having a son he called the f-word. But in a home with so much hate, these two managed to build a bridge of love between them. In many ways, Ellie loved Pinky more than herself, which is something she'd never admit in therapy, because it would probably result in (more) diagnoses and grippy socks. But it's true. The truest thing, actually.

It happened when Ellie was in the most awkward years of her life. About to go to high school, hitting puberty, feeling all these hormones and feelings, being conditioned to look pretty, thin, and soft. But not with Pinky. Pinky had their driver's license and drove Ellie right over the Golden Gate, arms out the window, screaming their favorite song in the car. *Gloria* by Laura Branigan. They showed Ellie a whole new world of possibilities, taking her to drag shows at AsiaSF, to protests outside City Hall, and to church services at Glide. They taught her there was more to life than "fitting in," that it was okay to be who you are, and even more, to take pride in that.

Life was (relatively) good until Pinky ran away. Things got really bad at home and Pinky went across the bridge, never to return. Ellie would take BART to go meet them. She saw the drugs, the parties, how things were rapidly declining. *But what could she do? Tell her parents?* They'd only lock *both* of them up.

The church service afterwards was the worst moment of Ellie's life. "Gloria in Excelsis Deo" was playing, like a sad, mutated version of their sibling anthem. During the opening processional, she walked down the main aisle, next to Gigi, which made things better. Uncle Timothy was right behind her, giving her nudges to smile more. But it's hard to smile when your favorite person in the world is in a coffin right in front of you.

Of course, her family was stone cold and emotionless, but Ellie couldn't hide how she felt. Her sadness (and her nerves) were written all over her young little tween face. It was the first time she felt the panic, the need to escape, to not be in the present moment because it was just too much. Every part of her being was telling her: *Red alert! Do not stay here. Run! This hurts like hell!!!*

As if things couldn't get worse, about mid-way down the aisle, she fell flat on her face. The whole procession stopped and every eye in the room turned to look at her, except her parents who, per usual, proceeded as if nothing happened, not looking at her, or ever, at each other. Uncle Timothy mocked her and Gigi helped her up.

The procession continued and it was at that exact moment that Ellie first felt herself floating above her body a bit, feeling more comfortable to not be fully in it.

Waiting at the altar, Father Tom braced for his moment to shine, as soon as the procession stopped at his feet. 'In the name of the Father, and of the Son, and of the Holy Spirit.'

Everyone made the sign of the cross except Ellie who was now floating up somewhere near the crucifix hanging from the ceiling. Uncle Timothy gave her a sharp elbow to the ribs, and she quickly made the motion - forehead, chest, shoulders - lagging behind everyone else, per usual. Gigi squeezed her hand as Father Tom and Sue locked eyes. Stan took notice—and so did Ellie. It's one of the few things she actually remembers noticing that day, besides the music and what happened next.

'We are gathered here today to celebrate the life of Paul Jones, son to Stanley and Susan, grandson to Gloria, brother to Elizabeth, and nephew to Timothy and Sally. We thank you, dear Father, for Paul's life, though taken from us far too soon. We lift him to you today, in honor of the good we saw in him and the love we felt from him. Please give us the strength to leave him in your care, in eternal life through Christ.'

Gigi gently stepped forward. 'Um, excuse me, but out of respect for my grandchild, can you please stop referring to them by their dead name? Their name is Pinky. Carry on.'

Everyone in the church held their breath as the showdown between Father Tom and Gigi ensued, a death match of the eyes, willing the other to be the next in the coffin.

From there, Ellie doesn't remember much because she was now floating up somewhere near the stars and the sun. The whispering started, Sue threw a Scene, and Gigi attempted to roll Pinky's coffin out of the church, refusing to let them be dishonored in this way.

Unsure what to do, the only thing Ellie could feel was this uncontroll-able urge to hug her brother, one last time, even as the chaos exploded around her. They'd lived their life together that way, finding love and fun amidst a family of tumult.

She put her hand on the coffin and then found herself hugging the wooden box. When her uncle tried to pull her off, as Gigi screamed at

Father Tom, and Sue screamed at Gigi, and Stan snuck away, and everyone watched on in horror, Ellie screamed too. A visceral, from the depths of her soul, howl. A mourning cry. Everyone stopped, turning to look at her as if she were the *crazy* one in this scenario, for the first, but not the last time.

Sometimes she wonders what would have happened if she did tell her parents the truth. If she did ask them for help. But how do you ask for help from people who have withheld their love? How do you ask two parents to care about a child they don't even accept? Or who only "care" when there's a camera involved? The saddest part? Ellie knew, from the time she was a little girl, that her parents just didn't know *how* to love her brother *or* her. Because the world hardened them and instead of opening, they closed. They became rigid and steadfast, clinging to old beliefs, as some life raft to save them from this wretched world. And it was not even really their fault. They were just conforming to a system that was never meant to allow anyone to be free, including them. So, they became the prison guards for their own children. The fact that their firstborn SON might not do the same as they did? Might refuse to sacrifice their life to meet the expectations of society? Refuse to bury their identity to be "loved"? Unimaginable to Stan and Sue. Pinky's freedom shined a bright spotlight on all the parts their parents stuffed in a closet, in drawers, in their memory, never to look at, because they didn't know how.

For Pinky, it wasn't the drugs that killed them. It wasn't the city or the wrong group of friends. Her brother could only make it so far. They got out of the cage but the guards still remained, in their mind. Pinky punished herself for wanting freedom. For being open and gay and queer and fluid and different and unapologetic about it. Except inside. Because inside was a little kid who still wanted to be loved by their mom and dad. Who wanted their parents to be proud of how brave they were to be themselves in a world that tried to hold them down. Instead, their parents were the enforcers, not wanting to be embarrassed, so they drowned their own child. Ellie watched. *What could she do?* They were her parents too. It was so easy for everyone to say afterwards: *See! We knew HE was troubled.* They might as well have spit on Pinky's grave.

In some families, a loss like that brings everyone closer together. But in many others, it doesn't. Especially not with her parents. The wedge only grew deeper.

But somehow, she hit the jackpot with Gigi and Austin. They could never replace Pinky, but they could remind her that the world wasn't as dark as it seemed. It actually seemed inevitable, really, that she and Austin would become so close through the years, their bond growing closer and closer and closer. It's like her brother said: *Okay, I'm so sorry love, I gotta go, but I know I can't leave you alone in this mess, so, here's a new brother, soon-to-be sister. Love them like you love me.*

So that's what she did. She refused to close her heart. She refused to become like her parents. She refused to let the world eat her, the way it did her family. She resisted with every ounce of her being.

Looking back, sometimes, she wishes she'd said something. Gigi and her talked about it, of course. But near the end, Pinky was hard to be found and the last thing they wanted was to call the cops on them. *God forbid Uncle Timothy and his buddies were on duty.* He would have shown his nephew "what's what." *Shudder.*

So, ultimately, Ellie did nothing. She said nothing. She watched and waited. And when the day she knew might come, came, she only said those three words. *Bit sad innit.* The funniest part was: that's exactly what Pinky would've wanted her to say. And most of all, they'd want her to be a force of love in this world. To love people like them, and most importantly, herself.

45

'Isn't it weird that a weapon is used to symbolize falling in love? Like the only way to be happy in this world is to be violently pierced?'

Ellie has her nose and her big belly pressed against the glass, staring out at the Embarcadero, focusing in on Cupid's Span, the bow and arrow sculpture in Rincon Park, overlooking the Bay Bridge.

Moseby has heard this one before. They allow Ellie this downtime to settle in, humoring the small talk about San Francisco architecture.

'That's an interesting way to look at it, Ellie. What else would you like to discuss today?'

Ellie finally moves to take a seat, facing Moseby. 'Well, I've been thinking about this a lot. In my next life, I'd like to be a dolphin. Did you know that Robin Williams said that if he could have been any animal, he would have been a dolphin too?'

Moseby holds eye contact. 'That's certainly a coincidence. Anything else?'

'Nothing else, that's really all I've got going on.'

They both look at her belly as they sit in silence for about a minute. Moseby knows better than to speak. They know the awkwardness in the air will draw whatever's boiling to the surface out of Ellie. It's just a matter of waiting it out.

'Okay, fine. I'm pregnant and I'm keeping it.'

Moseby can't help but slightly react, a near flinch that only someone who is watching closely would notice. Someone like…Ellie.

'Ellie, I'm very aware. Do you have your birth plan in place?'

'Do you ever feel like some things happen in life and you don't really have a choice? Like it's destiny and no matter what you do, you can't outrun it?'

'Let's unpack that. What do you mean?'

Ellie stares out the window at the "love" sculpture, considering what to say next. 'I mean, this was bound to happen. I *knew*. I knew everyone would think I was crazy. But when I had the vision of having a baby and then, was lucky enough to meet you, I just knew it was going to happen. I actually think I've known ever since I saw that psychic when I was sixteen.'

'What did the psychic tell you?'

'I don't think I should tell you, you'll probably send me back.'

'I won't do that, unless you threaten to harm yourself or others. What did the psychic tell you?'

Ellie gazes off, staring out the window. 'She told me I'd become a mother because I was picked to have a child named Gloria who would be beyond the norms, a perfect balance of both male and female. It was the scariest thing anyone's ever said to me, because: a. I was terrified of becoming a mom. And b. everything with Pinky.'

Moseby hands over the Kleenex, in preparation. 'Why are you scared to be a mom?'

Ellie stands up, facing the window. 'Because my own mom is terrible towards me. She dressed me up like a doll ever since I was little and it was shocking to her that I wouldn't just be mute and look pretty my whole life. That I actually had feelings and thoughts and a personality. I got "lost" at Fisherman's Wharf when I was four because Pinky wanted to see the sea lions so my mom just left me alone AS A TODDLER, pleasantly enjoying her time with her favorite child on the other end of the pier. I couldn't find them and luckily, a store manager found me and held me up above the crowd, screaming into a megaphone: *Who owns this girl?* Literally, *anyone* could have claimed me. Pinky spotted me. They were six years old at the time. Six! Afterwards, my mom grounded me, said it was my fault that I got lost, and took away all my favorite stuffed animals. The next week, my brother got lost too, at Neiman Marcus, and my mom tore apart that store, searching for Pinky but she hadn't even *looked* for me. And now, Pinky is gone and that's become one more reason for her to hate me more than she already did. And it's only gotten worse the older I get and no one even acknowledges what happened with Pinky, no one will talk about it, they all just go on as if she isn't dead. So yeah, becoming a mother is the scariest thing I could do, because I do not want to end up like mine and I also can't handle losing another person I love.'

Moseby sits back, allowing Ellie to breathe. This is the breakthrough they've been waiting for. Time to razzle dazzle their favorite client.

'First of all, I believe your child will be special, like all children are, and I believe you are special, Ellie. I'm very sorry about your mom and I'm even more sorry about Pinky. And I'm sorry this world doesn't understand people like you. But maybe this relationship, with this beautiful child that you get to raise any way you'd like will be the most healing experience for you? Maybe you will become the mother you always wished you had. Wouldn't that be a beautiful gift to give to this world? And most importantly, yourself?'

The realization seeps into Ellie as Moseby speaks. And new thoughts start forming, like beams of light finding their way into the darkest caverns of her brain. *Maybe her past doesn't define her future? Maybe things can work out, for once?* Huh. She never thought of that before.

46

39 weeks. Her baby is fully cooked and delivery time is nearly here. No one told her how the last bit is the hardest. How she feels like she's walking around with a giant moving pimple on her midsection that's ready to pop. Sleep is sporadic and not easy to come by either. Instead of fighting the insomnia, her new ritual is to do the only thing that relaxes her (outside of music and drugs). Star gaze.

Wandering into the fancy backyard, circling the pool, she turns her eyes up to her favorite friends - the ones who never let her down. Dipping her feet in the water, she scans the sky, landing on the star she was hoping would be there. It always is. And every time her eyes land on it, the same emotions come over her. Before she can overthink, she starts talking.

'I wish you could see this house. You would FREAK out.'

Ellie keeps waving her feet in the water, delaying the inevitable, trying to skirt out of what she knows she needs to say.

'Fuck, I miss you so much and then a part of me is so mad at you for leaving me here with all of them and then I feel like an asshole for that. But there's not a day that goes by that I don't think of you. And trust me, sometimes, I try not to. No offense to you, it just hurts. But there's always something, a song, a shirt you stole from my closet, an old note, a keychain you gave me. It's like everywhere I turn, there you are. And I don't know what to do with that. Because all I know is that there is a hole so big inside my heart with your name on it. And I try so hard to make it go away, but then I feel like I'm losing you forever and I don't know what to do. I just hope, wherever you are, you're happy. I honestly hope you are having so much fun and really, that gives me a bit of FOMO because I like having fun with you the most. Mostly, I just want you to know I'm sorry. I'm so sorry, for everything. I should have done more. Anything. I wish I could go back and protect you and I'm sorry that I messed up.'

The frog returns in her throat and as if on cue, her phone buzzes—and it's the only person in the world she'd talk to in this current state.

Actually, sometimes it feels like her grandmother has an emotional tracking device on her, always knowing the exact moment she needs her the most.

'How's my favorite Grammy doing?'

Exhausted, Ellie doesn't sugarcoat it. 'Not the best, Gigi. I'm sitting here, feeling like an overinflated balloon, I can't sleep, and I'm crying about Pinky.'

'Oh dear, you're right on track then. Before every birth, the mother must cleanse and you're doing just that. To be honest, I'm happy to hear you're in this state. I kept thinking, when is this little rose of mine going to let her petals fall?!?'

'Can I tell you something?'

'Yes, cross my heart, hope to die.'

'Gigi!'

'Oh, whoops, sorry dear. Cross my heart, hope to exist for eternity.'

'Thank you, that's better.' Ellie hates when Gigi talks about her death. Her grandmother has tried to walk her through her place in Berkeley, earmarking what's valuable, but every time, Ellie finds an excuse to deflect the subject.

'What's on your heart, Grammy?'

'I think this *was* all a big mistake. Maybe the headlines and the newspapers are right. I could do adoption, like Aunt Sally suggested-'

Gigi cuts Ellie off, something she never does. 'I'm sorry, love, but I have to do this. You know I despise talking over you, your voice is powerful and needs to be heard, but right now, you're in the first stage of labor no one talks about. The emotional spiral. So, I'm gonna tell you this and I'm gonna tell you this once.'

Ellie is silent on the other end, shocked by Gigi's sudden seriousness.

'Don't you ever, and I mean ever, doubt who you are and who you came here to be. Not a priest, not a parent, not a teacher, not the goddamn President, hell, not even me, and certainly not your uncle - no one can take your truth unless you let 'em. And your truth, my sweet one, is you're far brighter than most anyone in this world, and because of that, people will try to take your light away. Don't let 'em. Do you hear me?'

Ellie wipes her tears from her eyes. 'Yes.'

'I know this might be too much but I'm going to say it anyway. Some things in life, we can never escape, even if we try. There's nothing you or I can do about Pinky, about the shockwave you've had to endure during your pregnancy, none of it. Some things were written in the stars, in the music of the universe, long before we were ever born. Want to know what we *can* do?

Ellie can only nod, and energetically, Gigi senses it.

'We do the best we can. If I know anything, Pinky is with you every step of the way. And nothing in this world has made me happier than watching you become a mother. And I'm not saying that in a gross patriarchy way. I mean it in the Great Mother Goddess way. You are loved, you are protected, and being your grandmother has been the greatest honor of my life. Now, go get a glass of water, lay down in that gorgeous hammock, and take a star bath. I promise, this will all change soon. Everything is temporary and I love you to Venus and back and then some. Now, go rest.'

With that, Ellie crawls in the nearby (luxury) hammock, letting her eyes slowly close as she slips into a vivid dream, only this one is a bit... different.

* * *

She finds herself sitting front row at The Fillmore, the place she first saw Alanis Morrissette, sneaking in as a teen. But now, she's in the future, she's older, and she's so excited for the performance to begin. The lights turn low and a palpable hush of anticipation pulses through the packed venue. As the lights turn up, in a dazzling show, the announcer shouts:

'And now...we have the one, the only...!!!!!'

A beautiful human struts on stage, and Ellie is cheering them on with her whole heart. Everyone is. The whole room is pulsating with joy. She's never felt so much love in all her life.

The performer takes a few bows, before grabbing the mic. 'Thank you, thank you so much. I'm so excited to be here with you all tonight. We have a very special show planned but before we start, there's one very special audience member that I want you all to meet.'

Older, wiser, more beautiful Ellie is vigorously giving the "cut-throat" signal, begging not to be introduced.

'Everyone, the woman who groomed me for this place, my mother!'

47

'O-M-G, you slept outside?!?! I thought you'd run away to Tijuana. You truly almost gave me a heart attack.'

Austin is standing over the hammock, mimosa in hand.

Ellie blinks her eyes open. 'You're drinking? What time is it?'

'It's 5 o'clock somewhere and judge lest ye be judged. It's time to go, we're going to be late.'

'I had this dream. I think Gloria is going to be like you.'

Austin gives her a look.

'I don't know, I just have this feeling.'

'Wouldn't *that* be a miracle?! Now, get up! You're going to get hypothermia out here, I can already see the signs.'

No one is more freaked out about the labor experience than Austin. Their dials have been turned up to the max, embodying the energy of a mountain lion whose den has just been discovered. In a weird way, it makes Ellie feel extra protected. Like Austin will chew someone's face off for her. *Very sweet.*

A full breakfast is waiting in the kitchen, one that her bestie has clearly been working on for hours, with a cup of her favorite hot cocoa waiting by her place. *This* is what family feels like and Ellie is grateful for it.

'I added some ayurvedic herbs to increase your *Kapha* element. That's grounding earth and you need it because you're a reckless lunatic who sleeps outdoors.'

'Thank you chef. This food looks amazing.'

Blushing, but also reveling in the affection, Austin chases more compliments. Words of affirmation are their love language.

'No, it's not.' *Bloop.* They're fishing for more.

'Um, yeah it is. And so is this place. I mean look what you've done!'

Ellie dramatically gestures to the room around them, glammed out *to the max* with decor, cute quote signs, and personalized hand towels. Like a Pinterest board on crack. Austin is fantastic in the kitchen (and the bedroom), a multi-talented homemaker with skills that come as naturally to them as styling their hair.

'You literally made all of this from scratch. How long did this even take you?'

'It's nothing, really, I knew we'd get to be roomies again one day, so I've just been saving up a few things for a while. Don't make fun.' The truth is Austin has been stockpiling arts and crafts for months on end, working overtime like an elf with endless access to pixie sticks.

'See, I could never do that. I don't have the patience. I'd much rather be like you.'

They act shocked. 'Yeah *right!* You are so much wiser than me.' *Bloop, bloop, bloop.*

Posed like the thinker, Ellie continues. 'Do you have any Pisces place-ments besides your Sun? I'd love to take another look at your birth chart.' Austin's eyes are lit up like a Christmas tree, so she carries on. 'You handle conflict *so much differently* than I do. I wonder what planet rules that, remind me to ask my spiritual advisor. I mean, I get so angry, which you would think was a Scorpio thing, but it's really because my Jupiter is straddling Capricorn and Sag, meaning when I care, I really fucking care and I will express my anger. *Loudly.*'

'Yeah you do, girl. No one is denying that.'

Ellie cracks a smile. 'Watch it or I'll make you wear that fat-shaming postpartum T-shirt from Melanie. But truly, you just have a way of being so soft and making everything so pretty. And special.'

'We all have our strengths.'

'I wish I could make life as beautiful as you do. I mean, what's the last thing I've created lately, aside from chaos?'

Right on cue, as if the universe does indeed have a sense of humor, Ellie's water breaks all over the gorgeous marble floor.

part five:
the incarnation

48

'THERE'S A BABY ON THE WAY HERE, PEOPLE! WATCH OUT! MOVE PLEASE, NEW LIFE COMING IN HOT!!'

By some miracle, in under thirty minutes, Bertha managed to get across the Golden Gate and to the E.R. Even though Ellie had been going to UCSF for check-ups, she made the executive decision to give birth at the hospital in Marin; ironically, the one she'd previously been locked up in. She figured the press wouldn't expect her to go there, plus she feels more secure just knowing Maisie is in the building.

Austin is handling this moment exactly as Ellie knew they would. Shoving people out of the way, dramatically busting through hospital doors, screaming at anyone in sight. Gigi isn't answering her phone, something which happens *never*. This is the one and only time Ellie is too distracted to care. By the time she gets assigned a room, Austin is (also) in a state of (phantom) labor. As Ellie focuses on her breathing exercises, her bestie rolls all over the room on the birthing ball, giving it a ride like it's never had before.

Of course, Austin has also prepared a plethora of decorations for this moment. As they roll about, they adorn the room. *The Chronicle* story about the baby shower blew up and ever since, Austin's event planning business has taken off faster than some tech giant's unnecessary space rocket. They've been carefully preparing for the birth for weeks now, ready to make this an experience the baby will never forget. Little do they know, newborns can't see color until like five months, but Ellie didn't have the heart to tell them that. *It's the thought that counts.*

'Will you keep calling Gigi? She's not answering me.'

In their best *Mrs. Doubtfire* impression, Austin dramatically replies, 'Not to worry dear, help is on the way!' as they rush out of the room to track down Ellie's grandmother.

Everything moves so fast. The waiting room begins to fill up, with some people here for support, others for the chance to go viral (again). Pete,

Miserae, Uncle Timothy, Sandra, Aunt Sally, but no Father Tom, as that would be *horrible* press for the church. Not one to miss a dramatic moment, Sue attempted to join in the birthing experience, before being quickly escorted to the waiting room, after Ellie's blood pressure spiked.

As Mr. Jones enters the Labor & Delivery lobby, shockingly with Ted by his side, Miserae waves them over to the seats next to her and Pete, while Uncle Timothy gives them each the stink eye. Luckily, Ellie's friends are *fully* aware of the homophobia that runs through her bloodline. *But that ends today. No more passing down hate.*

There's an obvious sense of chaos in the air, as Sue looks out the window, spying on the media swarming outside.

Uncle Timothy joins his sister. 'Look at this circus.'

'I know. What a mess.'

'We're still on? The plan?'

Sue turns her head towards her brother like a soap opera star. 'Yes. This is *my* grandchild, here. We need to protect him. Or her, if fate decides to curse me again.'

Uncle Timothy nods. 'Don't worry, I've been praying this little fella has a penis too.'

Across the room, Sandra is laying paper towels on the waiting room seat, refusing to let her leather Hermès pants touch polyester.

Uncle Timothy elbows his sister, gesturing towards his wife. 'You know what they say? Life's a bitch and then you marry one!'

As Sue nods in agreement, Pete and Miserae can't stifle their laughter. Ellie's uncle is a real-life, precautionary meme, and they're here for it.

* * *

In the labor room, as Ellie is in the throes of healing her ancestral line, hoping to birth another progressive into the world, she can't stop screaming expletives at the top of her lungs:

'Fuckshitballsackhomiehopperassholerepublicandamncrapbloodyhellhol
ycowtwatdickhead'

Just a verbal rampage, every swear word under the sun. Oddly enough, chanting curse words puts her into a deep, hypnotic flow state. However, her choice of words makes all the footage Austin is filming totally unusable for social, but that's okay. This is the craziest thing Ellie has done yet, and they feel honored to have a front row seat (from beside her, not of the canal).

The doctor has remained mostly silent, letting Ellie do the talking, until now.

'Okay, one more big push Ellie. You can do this.'

'WHAT'S THE TIME?!?!'

Austin strokes her hair. 'Honey, just push. Time is an illusion-'

'TELL ME THE FUCKING TIME!'

The doctor looks confused. 'Ellie, you need to push right now.'

'THE TIME!!!' As she screams her final request, another cry joins the room. Like two voices that were meant to be synced, all along.

The birth time was 5:55pm. She set the intention to give her child the best birth chart possible, and it happened. *Something* worked out.

She is now officially a mother, there's no turning back. But she also can't stop thinking about her grandmother. *Sure, she's a free spirit, but she wouldn't miss this, would she?!* There's a chance she headed down South on a gambling streak. *But would she really do that? Now?*

Just as Ellie is about to drift off, she sees a faint shadow by the door. Make that three shadows.

The first one enters and doesn't say a word. He walks with gentle steps, slowly making his way toward her, giving Ellie a soft kiss on the forehead.

'Thank you for coming.'

Tears fill Pete's eyes. 'Ellie, I-'

She takes his hand and connects it with the baby who instantly grabs his thumb. Pete is in total reverence, and Ellie couldn't be happier than to have him here, right now. It's obvious that he is not the sperm donor, but it really doesn't matter. Because she knows Pete and Guy and Austin and Gigi will all love this baby, in their own way—and if there's anything she's learned, it's that love is *certainly* not bound by genetics. Actually, DNA has little to do with love. Plus, she's always loved *Three Men and a Baby*, so her child having multiple parental figures is a dream come true. *More is better than one, right?! Talk about ancestral healing!*

'Did you stick with the name?'

She nods.

'Good. I'm so proud of you El.' And with that, as if compelled by magnets, their lips meet again, and for the first time in this lifetime, there's nowhere else she'd rather be. Unfortunately, time does still exist and there are others waiting to see her. The shadows in the hallway start moving so Pete makes way for the next guest.

'I'll be back tomorrow.'

Ellie smiles, nodding in return.

Slowly, Maisie enters the room, beaming at Ellie and tiptoeing towards her bed. 'May I?'

Ellie nods as Maisie admires her newborn. 'You did real good here, kid. *Real* good.'

'Thank you. Funny seeing you here.'

Pointing to the ceiling, Maisie retorts. 'Better than up there.'

'True. Thanks for coming down.'

'Girl, I wouldn't miss this for the world.' As if a love bomb has exploded in the room, they exchange a genuine smile, no sarcasm included. Even Ellie can see the joy pouring from her face. Until Maisie notices being noticed and straightens up a bit.

'You have one more visitor, but I told him to wait a bit, I wanted some alone time with this cutie. Can I let him in?'

Ellie looks nervous. 'Did he say his name?'

'He didn't need to.'

A moment later, Mr. Jones sits in the chair at her bedside.

'Do you want to hold them?'

He waves his hands no, as he stands up and surveys the baby, then sits back down, casually crossing his leg over his knee, trying to hold in his emotion. His voice catches, giving him away.

'I'm so proud of you, Ellie.'

'Thank you. I'm proud of me too.'

'No, really, I mean it. This is...beautiful. To see you like this.' He takes a breath. 'I have a confession to make. I figured you'd find out sooner or later and I don't want you to feel duped or anything.'

'Oh no, I knew you were too good to be true.'

'I may have pulled a few strings...at the bookstore.'

'What?!? How???'

'I know Ted. Well, I more than know him. We've been together for a long time, it's just not something we advertise. We're from a different time than you, it was different for us, with our families and our work. Anyway, I told him about this wonderful friend I met named Ellie. I was going to suggest you apply to his store, but I knew you'd never do it if I told you to. So, imagine my surprise when he said you just came in, by chance! It felt like my prayers had been answered. When he met you, he knew it had to be the same Ellie I loved, the one with pink hair.'

'So, you got me the job?'

'No, you got yourself the job. I just asked him to give you a chance. And then a second chance, after the color-coding incident, which I actually found to be quite endearing.'

Maybe it's because she just gave birth, but something in Ellie has softened. She doesn't need to joke, she just simply says, 'Thank you.'

'It was nothing really, but I just thought, you know, you should know. In case it ever comes up because I'm sure we'll be seeing each other. A lot.'

'Can I ask you something?'

'Anything.'

'Will you be the guncle?'

Mr. Jones shakes his head, laughing. 'I thought you'd never ask.'

50

If only the rest of the world were so kind to this new life. The next morning, the headlines are alarming, in the worst way possible, on both ends of the spectrum:

CHRIST IS NOT (!!!) BORN AGAIN

WE STAN BABY JESUS NUMBER 2 - WHAT WE KNOW ABOUT THE FIRST OUTFIT

HERETIC STRIPPER BIRTHS BASTARD

OUR GODDESS HAS BROUGHT OUR SAVIOR TO THE WORLD! SLAY!

WHORE IS NOT (!!!) THE MOTHER OF GOD

DID THE NEW SAVIOR CANCEL GENDER? LET'S TALK ABOUT IT.

LOCK HER UP! NEW MOM LIED ABOUT THE RETURN AND WILL PAY WITH HER LIFE!!!

However, there was one shocking exception. As Ellie breastfeeds her child, waiting to hear back from her grandmother, she flips on the news. *Just to see.* The male reporter who did the exclusive interview with her flashes across the screen. His report is stern, serious…and apologetic? *Maybe hell hath frozen over.*

'Obviously, I'm aware of what's going on with the woman who sat in this chair next to me, Ellie Jones. And in good conscience, I cannot sit here and report on this story as if it is real news, because it is not. I cannot cover it, I won't be a part of it anymore, and I'm already concerned with the damage I may have caused in this young mother's life. In my place, when it comes to this story, I'll let my co-anchor here take over.' With that, he walks off the stage, shocking even the crew, who have never witnessed this level of integrity before in the newsroom. *What is this, church?!*

The moment of uprightness is, however, short-lived as the anchor beside him clearly feels a jolt of electricity run through her spine, eager to take down another woman and excited for her opportunity to shine.

'Well, that was, um, unexpected, but there's *a lot* of unexpected things happening today. So, let's get down to business here. What we have is a lost, misbegotten, mentally deranged woman claiming to be the mother of god—and we can now confirm that the baby was born last night and there's talk that the child is a male but will be given a female name. We are still awaiting confirmation if this child is, in fact, the Savior returned - or not - and based on the seriousness of this situation, local authorities are stepping in to decide who should have custody of this newborn baby, who just might be the Savior, after all. Let's take a look at the information we have been able to gather so far....'

The first eyewitness they nabbed was Austin as they were exiting the hospital last night, with a babushka on their head, trying to remain anonymous but failing, while pushing their way through reporters. It's also clear they'd hit the bottle.

'No comment, no comment, no comment, ouch! No fucking comment, okay?'

'Sir, there's rumors that you're the father, is that true?'

'NO COMMENT. And it's Mademoiselle, to you!'

'Is it true the baby will be given a girl's name, even though it's a boy?'

'Ew! Did I teleport to the 1950s? NO COMMENT.'

'Has the baby been seized by authorities yet?'

'That's not possible. Can the authorities seize you though? And like I said, no FUCKING COMMENT.'

Oh, god. Next came Austin's dad, Ray, standing in his Orange County driveway where he not-so-subtly set up an impromptu press conference, only answering the faith-based news organizations. He even propped up a wooden cross he wood shopped himself against his garage as a backdrop.

The reporters knew just where to start. 'What do you think of this HOAX?'

Sternly, Ray replies. 'I think it's atrocious and Ellie Jones needs to be punished. We don't take these things lightly and what she did, giving birth to that child and claiming it was the Savior, it's simply unforgivable. And don't even get me started on the gender and name thing.'

'Do you believe she is the mother of god?'

'Do I look like I have a hole in my head? I think the better question is: what do we do with this son of a bitch she created?'

'Do you believe we should forgive her?'

'Absolutely not. Tell her to burn in hell.'

Ellie can't help but roll her eyes as Ray walks away. *Some things will never, ever change.*

She turns the craziness off, just as Austin finally arrives, looking like they haven't slept. It's clear they kept the party going. Ellie nudges the water on her hospital tray over to her bestie and waits. She's still breastfeeding, which Austin is oddly hyper-focused on. *They must still be really drunk.*

Austin puts their hand on their chin, as if studying an Encyclopedia. 'How's that working?'

Ellie gives them a weird look. 'Fine. Why do you ask?'

'Don't hate me but I read up a bit, not because I don't trust you but just to stay informed and I learned that babies sometimes have a hard time latching.' They pull up their shirt. 'Like to the nipple.'

'Thank you for the demo, I've seen a nipple before. Not to worry, we're good.'

'Cool. Cool, cool, cool, cool, cool.'

'You're acting weird. Can you just tell me what you know? I still haven't heard from Gigi and I'm freaking out a little.'

Austin motions to twirl their hair, nervous as all hell, as Ellie gives them another concerned look.

Finally picking up on what's up, she slowly reaches for the remote again, waiting for Austin to react.

Innocently, she says, 'I just want to watch Brother Husbands.' Except Austin *knows* the new season doesn't start until next year. They try to call her bluff, and just as she's about to press the On button, they swat the remote out her hand.

'I'll be taking that.'

'What? Why? *What* is going on?'

'I guess anticipation is the worst part. By the way, have you landed on a name yet?'

Flabbergasted, Ellie can't hide her annoyance. 'Um, we've talked about this one trillion times. You said, and I quote: *'Iconic, I love the name, Gloria is perfect, there's no other name in the world I'd choose for this child, it is such a statement, bold, proud, based on icons. Never, ever change it, it's perfect.'*

'Not me going back on my word! I *did* mean that and obviously, I totally and fully support every one of your choices, even the questionable ones. Gloria is a gorgeous name, don't get me wrong. And very serendipitous, obvi. However, let's just say, hypothetically, that you had to pick a back-up, what would *that* name be?'

'Next question.'

'C'mon there has to be at least one other name you've thought about.'

'It's always been Gloria and YOU KNOW THAT. I just went through a rigorous psych exam to prove I'm not insane for picking this name. Why are you doing this? Would you like to test me too?'

Austin sits down on the bed next to their bestie. 'Sweetie, there's just a ton of backlash and some pretty scary theories being tossed around. This whole thing is going viral like nothing I've ever seen before, to be honest. And I don't think it's healthy for you. As one of the co-parents, it would be irresponsible of me not to at least attempt to protect you. And the child currently known as Gloria.'

'Like how viral?'

'250 million views on one video, more than Charli D'Amelio's followers. It's bad. *Really* bad. So about that second name option…'

Taking a moment, Ellie stares at the wall and Austin assumes she's fully dissociated, a reaction they prepared for. But instead, she sharply turns back, fully present.

'You know what? No. I'm not changing the name. Not my circus, not my monkeys.'

'I adore the inner power you're harnessing, so I'd like to triple confirm: Are you *sure?*'

Ellie gives them a hard look.

'Have I told you lately how pretty you are, INSIDE and OUT?'

'Can you please call Gigi? I need to know she's okay.'

'Yes, no problem. On it.'

With that, Austin leaves the room, without looking back. *Something is wrong and they're just not saying it.*

51

'Spell the first name for me. I don't think I heard it correctly.'

'G-L-O-R-I-A.'

The salty nurse can't hide her judgment. 'That's not a boy's name.'

Ellie's Scorpio essence and newly heightened mama bear instincts are kicking in. *Full force.* It's time to make the name official and she does NOT appreciate the resistance. Ellie counters. 'We don't know if this is a boy.'

'But we do.'

'But we don't.'

'You can't name him that.'

'Says who? You? And please stop calling them, him.'

'Pick a different name.'

'No.'

'I'll be back.'

Triumphant, Ellie sits up a little straighter in her hospital bed, knowing this is a battle of the wills that she will *not* be losing. The wheel of fortune has taken a spin and luck is finally on her side. *Not today, Satan!*

She casually flips on the screen only to be met with her mother's face. *Jesus Christ.* It's clear Sue has gone through glam in order to face the media in her hotel lobby. *Why is she still in San Francisco?* Her make-up team swarms around her, trying to ensure they won't get fired for a stray split-end or a lipstick smear.

'What can you tell us about your daughter?'

'Well, I'm not really the best source, she hasn't even called me yet, so...yeah, I don't know what's going on with her. I did lose my mother a few days ago, so it's been a tough week.'

Lost Gigi? Lost her *where*? Gigi doesn't get lost! At that moment, two male nurses strut in. She recognizes one of them from her last stay here. *Not a good sign.*

The most dominating one speaks. 'Miss Jones, you need more care than we anticipated. We're going to have to do a few more exams with you, and I want to be clear, it's looking like this might be grounds for a 5150. That's an involuntary psychiatric hold. We feel you may be gravely disabled.'

'Are you fucking kidding me? Is this about the name?'

The nurse comes forward, trying to grab her baby. 'Let me have HIM, please.'

Ellie has reached her last straw. This can't be real. She finally raises her voice. 'My baby is NOT A HIM YET! We don't know that! Stop calling them that!'

As the nurses approach her, she knows what's about to happen. Ellie gets that wild look in her eye, letting it all rip. 'You know the thing that really BOGGLES MY MIND is that the people who have the biggest problem with me being single and picking a name I want for *my* child...they worship a MAN WHO WAS SINGLE! WHO WAS BORN TO A SINGLE MOM! TALK ABOUT HYPOCRISY!! A DOUBLE STANDARD!'

The nurses move quickly to strap her to the bed, as Ellie freaks out, like déjà vu from the warehouse. Once again, she finds herself screaming bloody murder, as the cops enter and take her baby away, just like before. Only this time, it's very real and she screams louder than she ever has in her life:

'GLORIAAAAAAAAAAAAAAAAAAAAAAA!!!!!!!!!!!!!!'

The world goes white.

52

Gigi is dead.
A stroke while playing poker.

And Gloria is gone.
Taken by the authorities.

53

Ellie used to think her personal hell would be folding socks for eternity. *Wrong.*

The minutes melt into each other. *What is time, anymore?* Every second feels like one more turn of a torture device, tightening the noose on her life. She hasn't gotten out of bed for hours (days?), or drank a drop of water. And eating has fallen far, far off the table.

This time, her (padded) room feels less like a place of refuge and more like a prison. *What's the point in trying?* Nothing ever goes her way. And nothing can take this pain away.

First Pinky, and now, Gigi and Gloria, AT THE SAME TIME. *What atrocity did she commit in a past life to deserve this?*

Oh, and Austin too. They were so stressed out after having to lie to Ellie that they drank three mini-bottles of vodka in the parking lot and got a DUI on the way home from the hospital, landing them in jail. They tried to call Gigi…which obviously didn't work, so they buckled and called Aunt Sally, who simply replied: *MY MOTHER IS DEAD!* and hung up. Ellie feels comforted, in a way, to know she's not the only one being held against their will.

The only person she'll allow in her room is Maisie, and she has yet to (verbally) respond to her.

'Miss Ellie, I'm going to need you to drink this. And take five bites of this bread. I'm not leaving until you do.'

She doesn't move.

'Okay, I didn't want to have to do this, but I will. I have this letter. And I'm only giving it to you, if you do what I ask.'

Slowly, Ellie turns towards her favorite nurse. Her eyes lock in on the envelope with familiar handwriting on the front: *If.* She sits up for the first time in 72 hours, jamming the bread in her mouth.

———

Grammy,

If you're reading this, I'm dead. Physically.

First, a few details. The only memorial I'd like is for you, Austin, and Gloria to put on your Sunday best and enjoy a platter of popovers under the Rotunda. Be sure to smuggle the crumbs out for my swan babies at the Palace.

The Tahoe house has gone to the wolves, but the Berkeley house is yours. I suggest renting it out, hopefully to someone we'd like, and taking this time to be with Gloria and create a home that's yours, wherever you want it to be. My attorney will handle everything.

You're probably quite sad, which is flattering. Cry a little bit, of course, but please don't drown yourself in tears. John & George have been waiting for me. Oh, and your grandpa too. That cheeky geezer.

Guess what? The day you told me you were pregnant was the day the doctor told me I was going to die. It's the only time I've ever held the truth from you, don't be mad. But talk about manifestation, I couldn't have planned this circle of life moment better myself!

You are the light of my life, and I am just one star in your galaxy. Don't focus on what's missing. Look for me, I promise I'm there. And remember, there's always a way out.

Keep the faith,
Gigi

54

It's after 3am and Ellie still can't sleep. For the first time ever, she doesn't see a way out, of her grief, of her mess of a life, of any of it. She's been told she has only two options.

If she agrees to give up custody of Gloria, she will be set free, alone. *So, not an option.*

Or if she refuses to give up Gloria, she will remain locked up while her baby is taken away. *Also, not an option.*

Damned either way.

Trapped by the binary (yet again!), she's ruminating into the wee hours, looping the same (drastic) scenarios in her head, willing her mind to find the solution.

She knows she must stop the cycle of rumination but she can't. *For Christ's sake, she just gave birth and her grandmother died, on the same day!*

She does the only thing she knows to do: drops to her knees.

'Holy Mary, Mother of God, I rarely pray and I'm sorry for that. I know this is so cliché, to only come to you in a moment of crisis. I would promise to be better but we both know I won't be. All I have to say is…you know what it's like to lose a child. So please, I'm begging you with everything I am, I will be a good mom, I know I will. Please, I never ask for help, ever, from anyone, and now Gigi is gone and I'm here all alone and just please, help me. Please, please, please. I am begging you, with my whole heart, just…please.'

She shuts her eyes, when suddenly, she hears a noise by the window. She snaps up, looking at the clock. 3:33am.

The moment she reaches the windowsill, she hears the singing. Perched on the branch outside, chirping away. *A blackbird singing in the dead of night.*

Two memories come flashing back in her head, like lightning bolts.

Obviously, the Beatles song. Gigi's favorite. She looks down at her wrist, at the little blackbird, wings open, that Gigi had Earth Feather mark them both with.

But, also, the field trip her class took in 5th grade. When Gigi chaperoned and cut off the nature leader, pausing by a tree to let the class hear a blackbird sing and explaining:

You know what that bird is singing for? It's establishing a nesting area, letting all the world know they'll do anything to protect their babies.

She knows *exactly* what to do. Almost like Gigi's been preparing her for this moment, all along.

55

It's a beautiful morning in the psych ward. The baby deer, now grown, are drinking from the creek outside with their mother. Real flowers, sent by fans, sit perched by the open window, with the sun shining through, and a steaming cup of tea on the table.

Tapping her grippy socks on the cold tile, Ellie waits for the signal as she tries to tune out the faint chant of the protestors, coming from the window.

Maisie urgently busts in the room. 'Miss Ellie, we've gotta get things moving here, what do you say? No need to be alarmed but, um, it's time to go, girl.'

'I thought we were waiting until the shift change.'

'There's no time like the present! Stay calm, but those folks out there are creating quite the commotion, threatening to storm the place and WE ALL KNOW THEY'RE CAPABLE OF DOING IT! We need to get you out of here, NOW.'

The chanting from outside grows louder. Maisie hands Ellie the pass for the exit. 'I'll meet you at the bottom of the stairs. Godspeed, girl.'

Ellie nods as she watches Maisie leave. She peers out the window, instantly pulling back. Counting to ten (*one-Harry Styles, two-Harry Styles*), she peaks her head out the door.

There's only one nurse, preoccupied by the phone. She swiftly death drops to the floor, putting her skills from her previous occupation to good use. Army crawling her way to the door, she reminds herself how many times she's (successfully) done this before. Gingerly, she reaches one arm up to touch the pass to the sensor, cringing as the door makes a loud click as it opens. She glances behind her, making direct eye contact with a patient. *Fuck.*

He screams. 'Someone is ESCAPING!!!! Secure the perimeter!'

Fuckity fuck fuck fuck. Ellie knows there's not a moment to spare. She's on her feet before the guy can blink, another skill from her time on stage. She makes it to the stairwell before the nurse can react, hauling ass down the stairs with all her might, losing her breath as she nears the bottom. She hears a door open from up above and prays it's who she thinks it is...

'Didn't Britney have to do this too? We're following in her persecuted yet powerful footsteps.'

Austin rushes to her side, with a wig, a hat, and sunglasses in hand.

Ellie can't help but hug them. 'Are you okay girl?'

Austin quickly replies. 'Shouldn't I be asking you that?'

The besties continue sprinting down the stairs, jumping them two to three at a time. *This can't be good for her healing insides.*

'How'd you get out?'

'Mr. Jones bailed me out, goddess bless him. Obvi, *this* mama needs to cut back on drinking. But we'll deal with that later.'

They reach the exit, both filled with adrenaline, waiting for the next signal. As the door bursts open, Maisie rushes through, holding Gloria. She passes the baby back to the (rightful) mother, feeling the gravity of this moment.

'You're going to have to run as fast as you can. Stay low and wait for the all-clear signal when you get there.'

With that, she puts a hospital blanket over them as a cover, which oddly enough, makes them look a lot like the Holy Family. The besties take one look at each other, clutch Gloria a little tighter, and head out the exit, sprinting along the back side of the building, hauling ass to the creek. They can hear the chants coming from the front and they're almost to the water's edge when they hear someone behind them in the parking lot.

'Hey, you! Under the blanket! Stop!'

Austin turns to Ellie. 'Run.' They drop out from under the blanket, turning to face the tough guy from the crowd while Ellie continues on.

Austin puts on their most hypermasculine tone, maybe a little too deep. 'Sorry, is there a problem here?'

Recognition passes over the face of the mob men. 'It's him! The gay dad!!'

With that, a few of his buddies turn in their direction. Then, the whole mob starts looking their way. Austin has been through this once at Outside Lands and it did not end well. They clearly second guess their decision to be the "hero" in this scenario. Dying by mob is not their ideal way to culminate this lifetime.

But then, suddenly, as if guided by the Lord himself, the throngs of people part as Father Tom walks through them, like Moses splitting the Red Sea.

The mob falls silent as the priest nears Austin, in an extremely serious manner, looking like a pharaoh who caught his former captive, mid-escape. He clears his throat and projects much louder than needed as Austin makes the sign of the cross.

'Good day, kind Sir. Are you harboring any runaway mothers?'

'No, Father. Actually, funny thing, I was just on my way to Mass.'

The crowd intervenes. 'Liar!'

For the first time, Austin notices that Father Tom is as nervous as they are.

'If you lie to me, an ordained minister, you will go to hell.'

Austin takes a big gulp. 'Yes, Your Honor. I mean, of course, Daddy. FATHER.'

Father Tom does a lap around Austin, circling to carefully inspect them, until he swiftly turns back, addressing the mob.

'This man is a Believer. Let him pass.'

Austin begins to (slowly) back away, as they can't help but mutter under their breath, 'Oh my god, oh my god, oh my god.'

Father Tom softly whispers, 'Don't let these people hear you say that, they will burn you at the stake.'

Shockingly, the mob stays still, afraid to question the priest's authority while Austin stays steady on their slow retreat, like backing away from a grizzly bear.

Meanwhile, Father Tom waves everyone towards the hospital entrance. 'Nothing to see here, back to our post.'

When Austin reaches a far enough distance, they suddenly pivot into a full-out sprint, reaching the secret spot at the creek in record time. They join the others on board the fishing boat as Mr. Jones steers downstream, away from the hospital and towards the Bay. Quickly, Austin joins Ellie and Gloria, back under the blanket, huddling together, just to be safe. They don't need to be spotted (again).

Austin can still feel the adrenaline pumping through their veins. 'You will not believe what just happened. I never thought I'd say this, but I think I may have just been… "saved"?!'

part six:
redemption

56

Back in Seacliff, safe and sound in their (temporary) family room, Ellie and Austin are on the couch, the lights are dim, and Gloria is sleeping in Ellie's arms as she gestures towards the TV.

'Will you put the news on? Quietly.'

Austin looks at her, judgingly. 'What are you, a total masochist?'

Knowing she won't take no for an answer, they press ON, against their better judgment.

Immediately, the screen fills with headlines:

Savior Mom Breaks Her Silence

Lying Mother Comes Clean: The Savior is NOT Returned

CONFIRMED: NOT the Second Coming - Jesus Would Never Come Back to a Single Mom!

Holy Blasphemy: Unwed Mother Apologizes for Second Coming Drama

Angry Mob Won't Accept Apology Video - "Mother of God" Must Pay!

Austin looks at Ellie, shell-shocked. 'Oh my god, you did not.'

'I very much did. It was the only way out of this mess.'

They both turn to the screen as the reporter continues.

'You know this whole case has been a shitshow from start to finish, so we'd like to just play the video for all our viewers now, so you can decide for yourself, who and what to believe. The apology video is titled: "Addressing the rumors / my truth: so sorry for my eventful year." Here it is...'

Ellie's face fills the screen. She's crouched in the empty upstairs marble bathtub, clearly trying to secretly record this.

She's wearing an "Eat the Rich" T-shirt, which doesn't exactly help her cause, but is also a boss power move, given the opportunity she holds for reaching the masses. She has glasses on, no makeup, and takes a big sigh as she starts to speak, looking remorseful.

'Hey guys, I mean, hey all gender identities, Ellie here. Where to start? I wanted to finally address everything. Obviously, I handled this all wrong. Honestly, I've made many, many, many mistakes in my life. Anyone who knows me can tell you that. But how I handled this was probably my biggest one yet. The truth is I lied. I've lied many times before in my life but it has never turned out so…catastrophic.'

A soft sound of Gloria stirring in the background steals her attention away.

'Sorry, okay, so here's the truth. I was scared to tell my family that I was pregnant so I got nervous and said it was the Second Coming. It was the only thing I could think to say that would make them accept me and my baby. But it became this really big thing and it's gotten really, really out of hand and grown beyond anything I could have ever imagined.'

Austin can be heard in the background singing a capella, so she slowly gets up and shuts the bathroom door.

They turn to her in the living room. 'A warning would have been nice!'

Ellie gestures back towards the screen, eager for the ending, as the airing of the video continues. She mouths the words as they come out of her mouth on screen.

'From the bottom of my heart, I'm sorry to anyone I've hurt. My baby is not the Savior of the world, but they are the savior of *my* world. I never intended to insult anyone's faith. At the same time, I would never want *my faith* to dictate how anyone else can live and who they love. Maybe I'm doubling down here, but gender fluid and nonbinary people are actually the closest thing we have to god because god has no gender either. Also, people *think* they don't "get" gender ambiguity and fluidity, but they actually *love* it. Look at Prince, Freddie Mercury, Elton John, Lady Gaga, Harry Styles. Heck, even Jesus had long hair and a very pretty face, from what I've seen. They're all very popular and very, well, queer looking. I'll leave you with this.'

Ellie takes a long, final pause, looking like she might sneeze, until she finally delivers her closing statement.

'Do you know what god is, spelled backwards? I'll tell you. It's dog. I'm sorry, now please leave me alone, unless you like me, then thank you for the support, it means the world and you can follow my bestie, Austin, for updates and any events you may need planned in the Bay Area. Okay, but the rest of you, please forget who I am, I beg of you. K, byeeeeeeeeeee!'

The video abruptly cuts out as Austin instantly mutes the TV, trying to hold in their laughter.

'You are so weird, and I love you for that. It's not exactly going to calm the haters. But good on you, though, for standing up and taking some accountability. Plus, it's always important to raise awareness for our fur friends. Maybe Jonathan Van Ness will retweet!'

Looking genuinely concerned, Ellie sheepishly mutters. 'I haven't looked at the comments. Will you?'

'Yes, but before I do, I want to ask you a serious question.' Austin pauses, bracing as they ask, 'Are you *absolutely* sure about the name?'

Quickly shifting gears, Ellie looks exasperated. 'Yes. End of discussion, yes.'

Austin tries a different approach. 'You know I'm like the poster girl for gender fluidity, but I will say, this might be a little too much, too soon, for the world. I can't believe I'm even saying this but maybe just pick a more gender-neutral name for now and then let them change it later, if they want to. It'll save everyone so much grief and really put this to bed.'

The fire blazes in Ellie's eyes. 'You, of all people, should know, we don't know what Gloria's gender expression will be.'

'You're right. That is correct. *And* other people are going to say they *do* know, based on the genitalia. We want to turn *away* negative attention right now, remember?'

'But isn't this the one thing you are most passionate about, like, in life? The freedom to choose one's own identity? Why are you being so flaky now, when it actually matters?'

There's nothing that triggers Austin more than being called a flake. However, their reaction is different than usual.

'Honestly, I kinda feel like this is my fault. Like you're inviting in a world of trouble for Gloria, all on my behalf. And like, I just want you to know, I can fight my own battles and I don't need you to do this, just for me. As the godmother, I want to protect this child, just as much as you do. Oh, which is also why I'll be heading to rehab tomorrow.'

With that, Ellie slides her head down the couch, embracing her bestie. 'I'm proud of you.'

Austin dries their tears. 'Thanks, thanks. I wanted to tell you with a little Amy Winehouse dance number, something like, "They tried to make me go to rehab, and I said, YES, that's actually a great idea." But the routine wasn't exactly flowing. My creative well is low.'

'Well, it's time to fill it back up. And as far as the name goes, protecting doesn't mean conforming. We won't be accomplishing *anything* if we fold to what everyone else expects. And the online mob will find a new person to skewer, soon enough.'

Austin doesn't say a word. In an act that's wildly out of character, they actually show physical affection back, curling up next to Ellie.

'God, I wish I had a mom like you.'

SIX MONTHS LATER

57

With a newly dyed mane of pink, Ellie is doing her usual getting ready routine, only now, it's a little different. She pulls a sweater down over her nursing bra. As she applies liquid eyeliner in the mirror, she looks over at Gloria, watching them while she styles her hair in pigtails, then Gloria's too. She adds glitter to her cheeks and pulls slippers on her feet, instead of stilettos. She pounds her usual two glasses of water, ready for what's ahead.

On today, of all days, she never expected to be this joyful. *This might be one of the best days of her life, actually.*

Just last month, she shot a down and dirty stand-up special. Ironically, her first time ever on stage where she was clothed and paid beforehand! It started out rough, she bit it hard on her opener, trying to stay "on brand" with dog jokes.

'Has anyone ever had sex in front of their dog?'

The energy in the room completely dropped, like the last brick from the Titanic hitting the ocean floor.

'Okay sorry, wait, that came out *way* differently than I meant it.'

Austin can even be seen in the front row with a look of distress, mouthing 'what the fuck' at her.

'Alright, weird start, just for the record, I *don't* do that, I find it really weird and that's what I was trying to say. Sorry, I'm not used to being on stage with my clothes on.'

Uproarious laughter. Her career has skyrocketed since. To the point where she's been able to buy a house of her own, not in Seacliff, but overlooking the Presidio. *Not too shabby.* And today, she gets to host Christmas Eve, in another major upward spin of her good fortune.

On the other side of the state, down in Laguna Beach, the normies are gathered around the same table as last year.

Father Tom still believes the Bible holds the answer to everything, except when it comes to his relationship with Ellie's mom, the *only* anomaly. They have vowed to stay together, forever. *Or at least until the Vatican finds out.*

Even though Ray renounced his child publicly, he's been dipping his own toe into the waters of who he really is, inside. Unfortunately, so has Father Tom, whom Ray recently spotted on his favorite hook-up app, accidentally matching with him.

Aunt Sally has been (secretly) contemplating a permanent move to Tahiti. But her plans were sharply derailed when her (main) dog was diagnosed with an extremely rare blood disease that doesn't allow him to come into contact with any other animal or hard surface. She blames the diagnosis on her niece.

Sandra has been cheating on Uncle Timothy, also with Father Tom, who is certainly making the rounds in this family. But she goes to confession afterwards, every time, so it doesn't count.

The State of California finally put an end to the Freedom Ferry. Uncle Timothy is now working on an underground line of submarines where guns will be allowed. However, there have been issues in the test runs, as a few shots were fired, poking holes in the exterior, causing an emergency evacuation and sinking the entire underwater fleet. He and Sandra are talking about saying their vows, with Father Tom, of course.

There's no iPad this year—and that's because the trip to Mexico doesn't include everyone. Melanie is the only one at the all-inclusive resort, looking for her next sugar daddy, a vacation paid for on Stan's dime, of course, along with the profits from her new, genderless dog brand, *Abercombie & Bitch* - an idea sparked by her ex-stepdaughter, though she'd *never* admit that.

When it comes to her family of origin, Ellie never wanted to live a life with tension and fighting, and she finally realized: she doesn't have to. Even if she's the only source of unconditional love, that's enough.

As she enters the dining room, the guests are already gathering around the table, ready to eat. The room is bright and cheery, thanks to Austin.

The Christmas decor has a twofold purpose: to celebrate the day *and* of course, for social. Their party planning wait list has grown exponentially each day, so much so, that by the time they were out of rehab, they founded a combo party planning and interior design firm with six employees. *No more ab videos for money, only as thirst traps!*

Mr. Jones and Ted are sitting next to each other, now openly together, while Austin is sitting next to Guy, careful not to look like *they* are openly together. Although it's obvious they are both tempted. Maisie and Moseby both agreed to come too, with their respective partners. Even Miserae showed up. Ellie and Gloria take their rightful seats, as the queens at the head of the table, next to Pete, who helped prepare all the food, like a king.

Austin digs in first. 'O-M-G, this meat is delicious'

Ellie can't resist. 'That's what he said.'

Moseby responds. 'Haven't we outgrown that by now?'

Austin says nothing, signaling to Ellie that something is up.

'What's going on?'

They look nervous. 'Nothing, chill.'

'Tell me. No secrets at this table.'

Austin puts their silverware down. 'You know, you've always been so forgiving, that's what I love about you.'

Ellie puts her fork down too. 'What did you do?'

Pete deflects, checking in with everyone. 'Did everyone get enough?'

Mr. Jones replies right away. 'This is so great. You did a wonderful job, Pete.'

'I had lots of help.' He looks at Maisie and her girlfriend, who both smile and wave off the thanks. Their U-Haul pulled up at 7am, in typical wlw fashion, jammed with locally sourced ingredients, including two live chickens in order to get the freshest of eggs.

Austin scoots their chair back. 'Can I say a few words?'

Guy smirks. 'Do we have a choice?'

Ellie tosses her napkin at her baby daddy. They've developed a close co-parenting relationship, probably healthier than if they were actually together. She's a Scorpio and he's a Gemini, so astrologically speaking, it's just smoother this way. They're both committed to Gloria and to supporting each other, and it's working out better than either of them would have ever expected. Also, Ellie knows Guy has a crush on Austin and oddly, she ships it.

Austin blushes. 'I just have a little something to share, it'll be a lickity split thing. No big deal.'

They quickly pull out a projector from under their seat, shooting a re-assuring look to Ellie, telepathically promising her this won't be a clip of her bowl cut again. Instead, they silently press play, showing a clip of an old home video, only this time it's one from Gigi's house, of Ellie and Pinky opening gifts as kids, followed by a montage of pictures of her grandmother.

Initiating a seance in Muir Woods.
Protesting in the streets of Berkeley.
Leading the naked bike ride through the San Francisco streets.
Smiling, cheek-to-cheek, with Ellie, Pinky, and Austin.

After a few moments, Austin stands, raising their glass of kombucha.

'Well, someone famous said we must laugh, otherwise we will cry, so get ready to laugh my friends!'

Everyone is still silently sobbing. Not a dry eye at the table.

'I came across that video, a.k.a. I hunted it down and I just thought it would be nice to remember the ones who can't be with us here today. Anyway, I'll be honest, I've never been a fan of this holiday. It's always been so stressful and stuffy and commercial. *Consumerism, amiright?!* But this year, I have to say, I couldn't be happier than to be here with all of you, even you.' They look over at Guy, who waves the attention away but secretly loves it. 'So, if we can all raise our glasses. To the best-looking family of choice in San Francisco, if I do say so myself. Whatever you celebrate, cheers to you!!'

Ellie stands, clinking her knife to her water glass. 'I'd like to say a few words.'

Clearly a bit buzzed from their over-fermented drink, Austin blurts out. 'Is this the *Third* Coming?!'

Guy quickly retorts. 'To be clear, I AM NOT THE FATHER! *This* time.'

They clink glasses, holding eye contact a little longer than necessary.

Ellie smiles. 'Well actually, now that you mention it…'

Pete's eyes look like they're going to pop out of his head.

'Just kidding, I'm NOT pregnant, in a delusional fantasy or real life. I've got my baby fix right here.' Gloria coos in response to Ellie. 'All I wanted to say is I used to despise this day, like for years. Dreaded it, hated it, you get it. I'm not suddenly a huge fan, don't get me wrong, but I can now say, this year, I like it and I see the value in it. Not the monetary value, but the symbolism of gathering together to celebrate something humans have been celebrating for centuries. That even on the darkest day, the light always returns.'

As she sits down, everyone cheers, and the love can be felt in the room, like waves rushing in from the ocean. As if on cue, the celebration is interrupted by a loud knock on the front door.

Ellie glares at Austin. 'Did you do this?'

For once, Austin is clueless. 'No, I promise. Now, who could this be? Ellie, will you be a doll?'

Skeptical, Ellie gets up from the table and heads to the hallway. She doesn't even check the cameras, she just rips the door open, hoping whatever is waiting on the other side is good. A part of her, deep inside, wishes: *Maybe it's Pinky? Or Gigi?* One can dream. *Delusionally.*

She sees the signs first.

WAR IS OVER!
WAR IS OVER!
WAR IS OVER!

The children are each holding the classic John Lennon poster, the one he used during the Peace Campaign in 1969. As the chorus of voices start singing Gigi's favorite Christmas song (*Happy Xmas: War is Over* by John Lennon), everyone gets up from the table to watch on.

In case anyone had any question about who arranged this Christmas carol visit, the entire lawn is filled with kids dressed like the Beatles (in the early years, in suits, just how Gigi liked them).

Ellie doesn't know *how* Gigi prearranged this, but it doesn't surprise her one bit. Of course, she would do something like this, on a day like today, to make sure Ellie wasn't sad. To make her happy. To make her feel loved.

Somehow, this day has become not just likable, but her favorite. *Not that she would ever tell a soul.* It wasn't perfect and it certainly wasn't where she ever pictured herself, but somehow, it all turned out better than she could have ever imagined, for once in her life.

* * *

Later that night, curled up in bed next to Pete, Ellie is watching the news. *A habit she will break in the New Year.* Pete isn't paying much attention, as he types away on his laptop for his (suspicious) "government" job. Ellie knows better than to ask questions. She trusts him and against all evidence to the contrary, he still trusts her. The reporter on the screen looks tired. 'Well, folks, Christmas is finally here and even though many of us were hoping for the Second Coming this year, it turns out, we were lied to, once again, by another hysterical female. But in the Christmas spirit, as Santa would say, the show must go on. So, this evening, we bring you a highlight reel of the amazing work we've done this year, thanks to all of you…'

A quick sequence showcases the "great work" completed that year: harassing a very pregnant Ellie; putting duct tape between the openings of the fence at the border, ensuring no one can get through; chucking paper towels at people in flooded homes; chopping down trees for fun; gender reveals causing wildfires; droughts and all the glaciers melting; plastic islands and oil spills in the Pacific Ocean.

Pete looks at Ellie, gauging her reaction.

She deadpans. 'So glad I brought a child into this…'

'Really the wisest move you could have made.'

'I'm really like a visionary. A forward thinker.'

Pete takes her hands. 'I think you did the right thing. And I think Gloria is going to grow up and do amazing things.'

'Hopefully.'

'It really can't get much worse.'

'It probably can only get better.'

'That's what I love about you.'

'Whoa, whoa, whoa. What did you say?'

'Oh god, here we go. Bolt the doors, she's on the run.'

Ellie looks at him. 'I love you too.'

He tries not to make a big deal out of it, even though his heart is leaping over itself on the inside. 'Hey, can I ask you a serious question? What really made you pick Gloria?'

'Are you trying to get me to change it?'

'Oh god, no. You know I'm a full supporter. I'd even be willing to become the next Mr. Jones one day, if you'll have me. But I'm just curious why you fought so hard for it. I mean, you took a ton of heat for that, after already going through the ringer.'

Ellie thinks for a moment. 'Well, you know obviously the song and my brother and my grandmother and the whole ayahuasca thing, it all made me think, like, this is the right choice. But when the blow back started, I almost switched it. Until I looked up the meaning. And Gloria means "something you take great pride in. A magnificence, a great beauty." And it just felt right. And then, honestly, I saw another mom do it on YouTube. She named her child with a vagina Michael, so I'm not the first. This will be a trend soon, just wait and see. That's the real, honest truth.'

Pete softly kisses her. 'That's what I love the most about you. You're so real. Authentic. You couldn't be fake if you tried.'

Ellie feels a wave of guilt wash over her as she thinks back to all the appointments she's had, just in the past week alone. Getting acrylic nails, false eyelashes, a spray tan, her hair dyed. But she doesn't want to deflect Pete's compliment. She's done swatting away his affection and she knows what he really means. Also, she's promised to only tell little, harmless white lies. She's sticking to the truth, mostly, from here forward, on the things that matter.

'Yeah, I mean now that I'm a *mother*, I prefer to be as *natural* as possible, really one with the Earth and stuff. Granola, if you will.'

Pete leans over and kisses the middle of her forehead, again, and Ellie actually enjoys it, while also wondering if he can feel the Botox?

Actually, this moment of tenderness, of vulnerability, opens something inside her. She feels her eyes start to well up, immediately turning to her nightstand, pretending to look for her Gua Sha stone.

Pete hears her sniffles. 'Babe, are you okay?'

Ellie digs through her bedside drawer, making a mental note to clean it out later. 'Yeah, yeah, sorry, I just am so committed to my self-care these days and I need to find this face stone thing…' The tears are pouring down, like a waterfall that can no longer be contained.

Finally, after an awkward full minute, she's composed herself enough to turn back and face Pete.

He looks at her, looking like he may burst into laughter, which immediately puts Ellie on the defensive.

'Why are you laughing at me?'

'Babe, I know you were crying.'

'Honestly, I wasn't. I'm dedicated to my facial routine and I'm sorry if that's a problem for you. We can talk about it in therapy.'

'Yes, you were. It's okay.'

'I seriously wasn't.'

Pete smiles. 'Remember, no more lies?'

She looks at him, begging him not to hold her accountable. Finally, his laughter pours through.

'Okay, just do me a favor. Go look in the mirror.'

Ellie throws the covers back, stomps over to the bathroom vanity, takes one look at her reflection, and starts laughing so hard she cannot breathe as she hears Pete doing the same from bed.

Her face is streaked with literal tears, as her spray tan from this morning has obviously not fully set. It looks as if Jackson Pollack splattered on her cheeks in a tanning booth.

Not wanting to shame her too much, Pete knows what will really make her day. 'Do you want to go for a soak? Wash those tears you're *not* crying off?'

Ellie's new home doesn't have a pool, but it has a hot tub on the downstairs balcony, overlooking the city lights as they shine at night. Her and Pete love taking a late-night soak down there and doing what they do best: laughing with and at each other. Being with him now, it's like the opposite of where she was a year ago. Pete still shows up, still tries, and mostly, he understands. And she does too. He's generous with her, giving her the grace the rest of the world hasn't.

As Ellie and Pete dip in the steamy, bubbling water, the back door opens. Austin quietly approaches them, holding Gloria.

'Sorry, I just couldn't sleep and I heard this little one and by that, I mean I picked them up and carried them out here and I know I'm not supposed to do that but I just love holding them, so I thought I'd just come down and…'

Ellie lightly splashes them. 'Get in here!'

Austin sits on the edge of the tub, in a bikini and a shawl, dipping their feet in, watching the stars while bouncing Gloria on their lap.

For a moment, Ellie looks up and finds the star she usually looks for. The one for her brother. And the new one, the one for Gigi. For the first time, in a long time, she realizes there's absolutely nothing missing anymore. She knows what the stars want for her. Because before long, she'll be up there too, so she might as well enjoy what she can while she's here. And now, she's got a kid to raise in this crazy world. One more soul to make this insane place a little brighter. And maybe she *is* crazy, but isn't that a good thing in a world like this? *Don't you have to be a little crazy to live here?*

Pete comes up behind her, wrapping his arms around her. 'The stars are beautiful, aren't they?'

acknowledgements

I am deeply grateful to the following groups, organizations, people, and pets who made this book possible:

Laura Branigan, for "Gloria" and Kathy Golik, her legacy manager, who saved the day (and this novel). Right after January 6th (yes, *that* one), Kathy shared the following public statement: "It's absolutely appalling to hear "Gloria" being played in the background of a widely circulated video of Pres. [name redacted]…given the tragic, unsettling & shameful happenings that occurred at the US Capitol." I wrote Kathy an email, thanking her for her public denouncement because I was working on a novel inspired by Laura's song. She responded saying she would be delighted to one day read it. So, I kept writing.

Gloria Steinem is not only Ellie's idol, but mine too.

Joyce Arnowitz, for loving the title and offering consistent support, love, and encouragement.

Kristin Hanggi, for believing in Ellie's story and helping me put the idea to paper in the early stages.

Carollyne Corner, for reading the first chapters and encouraging me to keep going.

Nichole Young, for reading an early draft (while on vacation!) and sharing excellent feedback.

Rob Bell, for teaching me how to share a novel with the world, with total freedom. A deep bow.

Marlee Grace, for hosting Flexible Office, a supportive space where I was able to write and edit in community. And for just being them.

Faith, Bella, and their team who supplied me with enough hot chocolate to finish this book.

Diane Wallin, for promoting my books more than anyone else; I'm eternally grateful.

Jenny Jones, for being the kind of person and creative I want to be when I grow up.

Judith Lomas, for creating a peaceful refuge where I could finish this book.

Rosemary Matulich, for being such a wonderful mother.

Lindsay Wallin, for your friendship and support.

Julie Noble, while I wrote this book, she became a mother, while being a dedicated teacher (in a pandemic), and she inspires me every day.

Haley Shoaf, for being the embodiment of everything this book is about.

Tula, for spending many, many hours of her life patiently cuddled up at my feet while this book was written.

My grandparents, for watching over me.

Rylee, Tommy, and Keira, I love being your auntie.

Anytime I doubted why this story needed to be told, I remembered: it's so the people in our lives, especially the children, will feel free to be who they are.

And to you, dear reader. With all my heart, thank you.

a special tribute

During the writing of this book, my grandmother's sister, Dorothy McMahon, passed away. She was born on the same day as Martin Luther King Jr. and lived into her nineties. She loved art, studied at the Art Institute of Chicago, and was a very talented painter.

Aunt Dorothy was notoriously labeled as the "crazy aunt." I was told she was mentally ill, but no one really knew why. It wasn't until I was older that I learned what happened to her.

Dorothy was born to poor Irish immigrant parents who had just arrived in Chicago, between the Great Depression and the Second World War. Shortly after her birth, her father ran away, abandoning the family. As a child, Dorothy worried about the health of her remaining parent, her mother Bridget. She said a novena every single day, praying that she wouldn't lose her mother too.

Her first panic attack happened in high school, and she was promptly sent to a doctor who told her to "never tell anyone." Without support or treatment, her anxiety got worse, and so did her depression. Eventually, she ended up receiving electroshock therapy. She spent the rest of her life dealing with severe mental health issues.

The stigma around mental health is that it is a personal fault, when the reality is it's usually a symptom of a much larger, deeper problem in the world around us. Inevitably, the people who are sensitive, gifted, and feel deeply, like my great aunt feel the effects of the unjust systems around us, the most.

I got to celebrate my aunt Dorothy's 90th birthday with her. We went to her favorite restaurant and ate pie. When my grandmother died, I was so sad, and she told me: "You can't die with her." She reminded me there was still life, after death. Dorothy later died in September 2022. I like to think she's free now, from all the judgment and pain. I'm forever grateful for her soft, gentle presence in my life, and I will keep making my art, always with her in my heart.

Caitlin Elizabeth (she/her) is the author of *Everything in Between*, which was featured in BookLife's Indie Spotlight for Memoir. *Mother of God* is her debut novel. She has written other books as a ghostwriter. She studied film & writing at the University of Iowa. She lives in Sebastopol, California with her very friendly dog.

caitlinelizabeth.me
@caitlinelizabethwriter

www.ingramcontent.com/pod-product-compliance
Lightning Source LLC
Chambersburg PA
CBHW020151310726

48970CB00006B/2095